*gymnasium
體育館, 健身房
專培養升高中,大學的精讀培養高級中學 歐洲較多,院小學
Secondary School

PART 1

1. (D) (A) Some people are in a gymnasium. * v+ing 規划
   (B) Some people are in a bank. 在銀行裡 ① open+ing → opening
   (C) Some people are in a supermarket. 市場, 超市
   (D) Some people are in an airport. 機場 ② use+ting → using 燕發音的e去掉+ting

正在準備一些食物
2. (C) (A) The man is preparing some food.
       洗一些碗 ③ sit+ting → sitting
seat   (B) The man is washing some dishes.
v.容納   (C) The man is making some copies. → sitting
使就座(背動), 主動用 v+ing的變化(圖) ④ tie+ting → tying, 先給雅去ie+ying
       (D) The man is tying his shoes. 鞋子, 重複旋tr+ing

3. (A) (A) Some people are seated at an outdoor café. 候診室
       (B) Some people are sitting in a doctor's waiting room.
       (C) Some people are standing on a bridge. 站在橋上
       (D) Some people are running on a beach. 海灘上奔跑

replace 更換 燈泡 在倉庫裡操作一些機械
4. (B) (A) The man is replacing a light bulb.
       operate 操作
       (B) The man is operating some machinery in a warehouse.
       (C) The man is making a delivery to a private home.
       (D) The man is opening a bunch of packages. 送貨到住家
   一束, 一堆, a bunch of flowers, a bunch of children

5. (A) (A) Some students are taking an exam in a large classroom.
       (B) Some students are watching a football game in a stadium. 佐考試
       (C) Some students are graduating from college. 體育館
       (D) Some students are talking in the library. 在圖書館聊天

* ride 騎乘,停泊 The ship riding close to shore 停在岸邊的船明天會啟航
6. (B) (A) Some tourists are riding a boat. will set sail tomorrow.
       (B) Some tourists are looking at a map. Don't cut in line?
排隊   (C) Some tourists are taking pictures. 拍照 Are you in line
└   (D) Some tourists are waiting in line. 排隊
wait   line up   We have to line up, it's the
stand │in line, queue up,   basic courtesy.
                     We queued for 30 minutes.

GO ON TO THE NEXT PAGE.

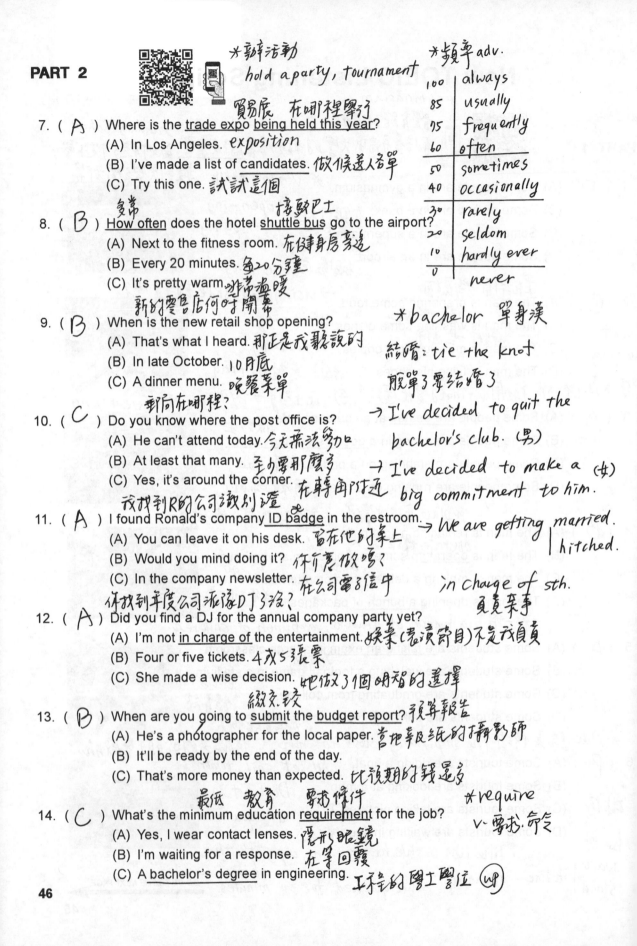

PART 2

*辦活動
hold a party, tournament

貿易展 在哪裡舉行

*頻率 adv.

100	always
85	usually
75	frequently
60	often
50	sometimes
40	occasionally
30	rarely
20	seldom
10	hardly ever
0	never

7. (A) Where is the trade expo being held this year?
    (A) In Los Angeles. exposition
    (B) I've made a list of candidates. 做候選人名單
    (C) Try this one. 試試這個

8. (B) 多常 接駁巴士 How often does the hotel shuttle bus go to the airport?
    (A) Next to the fitness room. 在健身房旁邊
    (B) Every 20 minutes. 每20分鐘
    (C) It's pretty warm. 非常溫暖

新的零售店何時開幕

9. (B) When is the new retail shop opening?
    (A) That's what I heard. 那正是我聽說的
    (B) In late October. 10月底
    (C) A dinner menu. 晚餐菜單

*bachelor 單身漢
結婚: tie the knot
脫單了要結婚了
→ I've decided to quit the bachelor's club. (男)

郵局在哪裡?

10. (C) Do you know where the post office is?
    (A) He can't attend today. 今天無法參加
    (B) At least that many. 至少要那麼多
    (C) Yes, it's around the corner. 在轉角附近

→ I've decided to make a (女) big commitment to him.

我找到R的公司識別證

11. (A) I found Ronald's company ID badge in the restroom.
    (A) You can leave it on his desk. 留在他的桌上
    (B) Would you mind doing it? 你介意做嗎?
    (C) In the company newsletter. 在公司電子信中

→ We are getting married.
hitched.

in charge of sth.
負責某事

你找到年度公司派隊DJ了沒?

12. (A) Did you find a DJ for the annual company party yet?
    (A) I'm not in charge of the entertainment. 娛樂(表演節目)不是我負責
    (B) Four or five tickets. 4或5張票
    (C) She made a wise decision. 她做了個明智的選擇

繳交.交

13. (B) When are you going to submit the budget report? 預算報告
    (A) He's a photographer for the local paper. 當地報紙的攝影師
    (B) It'll be ready by the end of the day.
    (C) That's more money than expected. 比預期的錢還多

最低 教育 要求條件

14. (C) What's the minimum education requirement for the job?
    (A) Yes, I wear contact lenses. 隱形眼鏡
    (B) I'm waiting for a response. 在等回覆
    (C) A bachelor's degree in engineering. 工程的學士學位

*require
v. 要求.命令

15. (A) Could you review this proposal? 你可以審查看一下這個提案嗎?
    (A) I may have time tomorrow. 我明天可能有空
    (B) Make a reservation, please. 請預約
    (C) Mike, Joe, and Anna.

*organic
adj. 有機的
不施化肥的

16. (C) What are the shipping options for mailing this package? 要寄送這些包裹有哪些運送選項?
    (A) Let's shut the window. 讓我們把窗關上
    (B) In the conference room. 在會議室
    (C) Overnight or three-day delivery. 隔日送達或3日送達

+food 食物
+fertilizer 肥料

17. (C) Would you care to try a sample of our new organic cookie? 你想要/喜歡/願意試我們新款有機餅乾的樣品嗎? 試吃品
    (A) I never knew that. 我從來不知道 (up)
    (B) That's a good point. 是個好點耶
    (C) Are there peanuts in it? 裡面有含花生嗎?

*estimate
n. 估價(單)
v. 估計. 評價. 判斷
to make an estimate

18. (A) Didn't you say Paulina Rogers would be on this flight? 你不是說PR會在這台班機上嗎?
    (A) She's sitting in row 15. 她坐在第15排
    (B) I'll look at the results again. 我會再看看結果
    (C) A repair estimate. 一張維修估價單

* 近視的
near-sighted
short-sighted

19. (B) Where can I find the printer ink cartridges? 印表機墨水匣
    (A) It's very fast.
    (B) Aren't they in the storage closet? 不是在儲藏櫃裡嗎? myopia
    (C) Usually every evening. 通常每個晚上

* 遠視的 hyperopia
far-sighted

20. (A) You've been to the World Trade Center before, right? 你之前曾去過世貿中心對嗎?
    (A) Ms. Wilson has.
    (B) These shoes are tight. 這些鞋很緊
    (C) I'm near-sighted. 近視的 (否)

long-sighted

* bill (英) 帳單
(美) 電話水. 信用卡單

check please! 買單(美)
Bill please! 買單(英)

21. (C) Can I get you something else or would you like the bill? 我可以給你什麼其他的嗎. 或是您想結帳了呢?
    (A) At the top of the hill. 山丘頂
    (B) We loved it. 我要再來杯咖啡
    (C) I'll have another cup of coffee.

Can we have separate checks?
I'll get my own check.

22. (B) What did you think of Sandra Park's job interview? 你覺得SP工作面試如何?
    (A) Yes, I met him last week. 是的. 我上週見到他
    (B) She seems highly qualified. 她看起來極度符合資格
    (C) At the job fair in Seattle.

GO ON TO THE NEXT PAGE.

47

23. (B) Could I borrow your stapler for a minute? 可以借一下你的訂書機嗎?
    staple 訂書針
    (A) The clock is on the wall.
    (B) Of course, here you go. 當然,拿去吧!
    (C) It was a great event. 真是個好活動

24. (C) How much does the position pay? 這個職位付多少錢?(薪水多少)
    (A) Mary is checking the inventory now. 正在檢查庫存
    (B) I prefer to live by the train station. 我較喜歡(寧願)住在火車站旁
    (C) $25 an hour.

25. (A) 我寄關於會議的資料給你了.有吧? *附加問句
    I e-mailed you about the meeting, didn't I? 前肯後否.前否後肯
    (A) I haven't checked my mail yet. 我還沒看信件
    (B) Near the bank. 在銀行附近 *forecast
    (C) He really enjoyed the experience. 他享受這個經驗

26. (C) 你知道行銷辦公室在哪個樓層嗎?
    Do you know which floor the marketing office is on?
    (A) The lights turn on automatically. 自動地
    (B) The forecast is out for December. 12月的預報已經出來了
    (C) They've moved, so I'm not sure. 他們有搬家.所以我不確定

27. (B) 下載 手機 app 應用程式
    I don't know how to download mobile phone applications
    (A) The road is closed. → Notarize (the) matrimony 公證結婚
    (B) It isn't difficult. Notary Office 公證處
    (C) A notarized copy of your birth certificate.
    確認過的.公證過的 → 確認過的出生證明

28. (A) When is the annual company charity event? 有機構認定過的
    (A) It's held every March. 每年3月舉行
    公司年度慈善活動何時舉行
    (B) Here's the conference schedule. 這是會議行程
    (C) About innovation. 創作.變遷 into new

29. (B) Has the print shop received our shipment of paper? 印刷店收到我們送的紙了沒?
    (A) That's a good idea. 好主意
    (B) Yes, they just confirmed it. 他們剛確認了
    (C) I prefer this painting. 我比較喜歡這幅

30. (A) 你想要 L or T 明天去產品發佈會嗎? ①發射②船下水②推出
    Do you want Louis or Tiffany to be at the product launch tomorrow?
    (A) I thought you were going. 我以為你要去(我暗示猜測原本未來會有此行動)
    (B) That lunch was delicious. What are you doing, John?
    (C) Sure, it was quite exciting. I'm going to the cinema this afternoon.
    Oh, I thought you were going to meet Mary this afternoon.

31. (B) Why are the clients coming so early? 客戶們為何這麼早來?
    (A) In the next building. 在隔壁棟
    (B) You'll have to ask Mr. Pruitt. 你需問P先生
    (C) Yes, please come in. *grant

*in the final stretch
home
home straight
= final portion of an activity

"撥款,同意
授予,助學金 = Students in the country receive
a grant from the government.

PART 3

Questions 32 through 34 refer to the following conversation.

明天撥款提案的狀態如何了?   你的影像報告準備好了嗎?

W : Thomas, what's the status on the grant proposal for tomorrow? Is your video presentation
    ready to go? 我在收尾階段了   只是有幾個…

M : I'm in the final stretch, Maryanne. Just… a… couple of…
你明有這次報告(UP)   會成就或摧毀我們   事情越到最後我越緊張

W : You realize this presentation will make or break us. I get nervous when things come down
    to the last minute. If we blow this, our wildlife preservation project is dead(下)

M : Of course. To be honest, the only thing I'm missing is the interview with the African hunter.
    You said you had a copy of the clip, but you never sent it to me. 坦白說,我唯一缺失的是
你說你有訪問片段(clip)的複本,但你還沒寄給我   非洲獵人的訪問

W : I thought I e-mailed it to you already. I'll re-send it as soon as I get back to my desk. 回到位子後

M : Thanks. It'll probably be a good idea to double-check the laptop in the conference room. 會再寄
    So after lunch, I'll make sure that the computer is properly connected to display videos.

再檢查一次會議室的筆電會是個好主意(你快去這麼做).
午餐後,我會確保電腦準接好
可以播放影片。

32. (A) What are the speakers discussing?
    (A) A presentation. 一個展演報告
    (B) A television show. 電視秀
    (C) A website. 網站
    (D) A bank loan. 銀行貸款

33. (B) What does the man say he is missing?
    (A) A signature. 簽名
    (B) A video clip. 影片片段
    (C) A password. 密碼
    (D) An e-mail address. email帳號

缺少 If we blow this,
如果我們搞砸了,我們野生動物
保育案就GG了

*preservation 1.保留.存.護
              2.維持

34. (C) What does the man say he will do after lunch?
    (A) Contact a journalist. 連絡一位記者
    (B) Review some data. 檢查一些資料
    (C) Check a computer. 檢查電腦
    (D) Write a proposal. 寫提案

The police are responsible for
the preservation of law and order.
治安

GO ON TO THE NEXT PAGE.

49

W : Hi, I recently came across a flyer for a community clean-up event next month. It said I should sign up to be a neighborhood captain here at City Hall. Who do I need to talk to about this?

M : Um, there's been a change in plans. Originally, the registration office was here, but it has been moved to the courthouse. We had new flyers made, but apparently a lot of the old fliers are still posted.

W : I see. Well, that's actually quite convenient for me. My office is across the street from the courthouse, so I can stop by this afternoon. By the way, if you have any extra flyers with the correct information, I could pass them around to my friends at work.

35. (C) Why did the woman stop by City Hall?
    (A) To claim a lost item.
    (B) To speak with an administrator.
    (C) To register for an event.
    (D) To file for a permit.

36. (B) Where is the woman instructed to go?
    (A) To a local park.
    (B) To the courthouse.
    (C) To a department store.
    (D) To a community center.

37. (A) What does the woman ask for?
    (A) Some updated flyers.
    (B) A building directory.
    (C) A map of the city.
    (D) A list of cleaning companies.

W : Hi, I'm calling about my credit card bill. I paid it online two weeks ago, but today I received a notice saying I was being charged a late fee of $25. That can't be right. I submitted the payment three days before the due date.

M : First, thanks for calling Tripp Financial and being a loyal customer. I can reverse that charge. You see, there was a problem with our online bill payment system, and late fees were mistakenly charged to thousands of customers.

W : Well, I want to make sure that my interest rate hasn't been automatically raised because of the late fee. Can you confirm that for me?

M : I understand. If you just give me your account number, I'll pull up your information.

50

38. (B) Why is the woman calling?
  - (A) To answer a question. 回答問題
  - (B) To report an incorrect charge. 回報一筆不當收費
  - (C) To close an account. 關閉戶頭
  - (D) To ask about a policy. 詢問政策

* boost
n. 推動、幫助、促進
a boost to their morale
對他們士氣的激勵

39. (C) What is the woman also concerned about?
  - (A) Frequent flyer miles. 常飛哩程數
  - (B) Membership fees. 會員費
  - (C) Interest rates. 利率
  - (D) Identity theft. 身分小偷 (偷取個資)

①一抬一舉
He gave me a boost over the fence.
抬我一把 翻越柵欄
v. ① 促進 boost a program

40. (C) What does the man ask for?
  - (A) A payment date. 付款期限
  - (B) A street address. 地址
  - (C) An account number. 帳戶號碼
  - (D) A password. 密碼

② 增加 The company boosted
提高 its sales this year.
③ 抬、推
give me a boost

Questions 41 through 43 refer to the following conversation between three speakers.

我想出了這個網站的新概念　這個想法會吸引更多的流量和刺激銷量

M : Hi, ladies. I've come up with a new concept for the website, and I think it will drive more traffic and boost our sales. Do you have time today to sit down and give me some feedback?

Woman UK : Unfortunately, this afternoon I've got a budget review meeting. But I'm free most of tomorrow. 不幸的是, 今天下午我有預算審查會議、但我明天大部分都有空

我今天行程也很滿。(行程塞團=滿滿滿)　10:00有空
Woman US : I'm booked solid today as well. If you want to meet tomorrow, I'm available from 10:00 a.m. until lunch. After that, I've got interviews for the open IT position. 新的IT職缺

M : OK, how about we meet tomorrow at 10 in my office? That will give me some time to tweak a couple of elements and bring the whole concept into focus. 整理一些部分　把整個概念理清楚

41. (A) What is the conversation mainly about?
  - (A) A website. 網站
  - (B) A sales report. 銷售報告
  - (C) A budget review. 預算審查
  - (D) A job interview. 工作面試

* implement
n. 工具. 手段
v. 實施. 執行 We need money to implement the program.

42. (D) What does the man want to do?
  - (A) Implement a new hiring policy. 實施新的僱人政策
  - (B) Begin a renovation project. 開始一個整修案 (整修案)
  - (C) Implement an advertising campaign. 執行一個廣告宣傳活動
  - (D) Discuss an idea. 討論一個想法

* solid
adj. 固體的
堅固的
穩固的

GO ON TO THE NEXT PAGE.

43. (D) What does the man say he will do before the meeting?
   (A) Read a resume. 看履歷 　　　　　＊revise
   (B) Hire a programmer. 顧用工程師 　　v. 修訂. 修正. 校訂
   (C) Print some flyers. 印一些傳單
   (D) Revise a concept. 修正一些概念

Questions 44 through 46 refer to the following conversation.

恭喜你完成了(簽訂了)Shelby案子　　　　我想請你幫個忙

M : Hey, Lisa. Congrats on closing the Shelby deal. Great job! Listen, I have a favor to ask.
   The Tokyo client wants to catch an earlier flight to New York for the weekend, so I need to
   meet with him this afternoon. So... I was hoping you wouldn't mind leading the intern
   training session at 3:30. I'll make it up to you, I promise. 希望你不介意主持3:30的內部訓練

W : I would be happy to, Jeff, but I'm having lunch with Dave Shelby to celebrate the deal. It's
   way out at his country club in Oak Brook, so I'm taking the rest of the afternoon off. Why
   don't you ask Tim? 吃午餐慶祝案子簽訂. 店在很遠的鄉村俱樂部, 所以我今天下午請假

M : I thought he was on vacation this week. 我以為他這週休假

W : No, he was working from home Monday through Thursday. He'll be here today at 10:30.
   And I'm pretty sure his schedule is clear this afternoon.
   我很確定他今天下午行程很乾淨(很空)

44. (B) What does the man want the woman to do?
   (A) Have lunch with a client. 和客戶吃午餐　　　　＊I'll make it up to you.
   (B) Lead a training session. 帶領訓練活動　　　　　我會補償你
   (C) Stay late. 晚睡
   (D) Work from home. 在家工作　　　　make up

   ①補足：We need $50 to make up the sum required.
45. (D) What does the woman suggest?
   (A) Switching offices. 換動辦公室　　②編造：The whole story is made up.
   (B) Taking a later flight. 搭晚點的班機
   (C) Canceling a meeting. 取消會議　　③組成：The medical team is made up of twelve doctors.
   (D) Asking a co-worker. 問別的同事

46. (C) When is the conversation most likely taking place?
   (A) On Monday.
   (B) On Thursday.
   (C) On Friday.　　　　　＊facility
   (D) On Saturday.　　　　n. 設備. 場所. 廁所

　　　　　　　　　　　　　我真的需要拿一些運動器材
　　　　　　　　　　　　　為了明天的壘球錦標賽

Questions 47 through 49 refer to the following conversation.
　　　　　　　　我在你們店裡有個儲存空間
M : Hi, this is Bob Reese. I have a storage space at your facility, and I'm calling because I lost
   the key to the lock. I really need to get some sporting equipment out of there for a softball
   tournament tomorrow.

W : That's not a problem, Bob. Come by the rental office and I'll loan you a copy of our key. We're open until 9:00 p.m. tonight.

M : What a relief! I'm on my way now. Oh, can I make a copy of the loaner key? It might take a few days...

W : We can talk about that when you get here, Bob. See you then.

47. (D) Why is the man calling?
    (A) To obtain a document.
    (B) To ask about a moving service.
    (C) To check on an order.
    (D) To report a lost key.

48. (B) What does the woman suggest that the man do?
    (A) Send her an e-mail.
    (B) Come to her office.
    (C) Bring a copy of an invoice.
    (D) Speak with the maintenance department.

49. (D) What does the man ask about?
    (A) Changing a schedule.
    (B) Finding an office location.
    (C) Selecting a moving date.
    (D) Making a duplicate key.

Questions 50 through 52 refer to the following conversation.

W : Hi, Simon. You know, everybody is thrilled that you transferred to the corporate sales division. I understand you've already opened a few major accounts. So... what do you think about the position so far?

M : I'm travelling a lot more than I thought I would, but overall, I'm very happy. This month, I've already met with a dozen engineering firms interested in subscribing to our network services.

W : Well, we have two new sales associates starting next week. So, you shouldn't have to travel so much in the future. You'll be able to concentrate on managing your accounts as opposed to landing them.

50. (C) What area does the man work in?
    (A) Personnel.
    (B) Engineering.
    (C) Sales.
    (D) Advertising.

GO ON TO THE NEXT PAGE.

51. (C) What surprised the man about his new position?
   - (A) The amount of paperwork. 文件處理的量
   - (B) The speed of the network. 網路的速度
   - (C) The <u>frequency</u> of travel. 旅行的頻率
   - (D) The long hours. 工作時間太長

*頻率 adv. 放 be V 後. 一般 V 之前
I am sometimes wrong.
I sometimes make mistakes.
放 not 之前. always/ever 例外
I sometimes don't make right decisions.
I don't ever make mistakes.
I am not always correct.

52. (D) What has the company done recently?
   - (A) Upgraded a system. 更新系統
   - (B) Discontinued a product. 商品停產
   - (C) Launched a marketing campaign. 推出行銷活動
   - (D) Hired new employees. 雇用新員工

Questions 53 through 55 *refer to the following conversation.*

新的信用部門

M : Yes, good afternoon. May I please speak with Donna Carlson? This is Rich Tilley from the consumer credit division at Mega National Bank. see

W : Hi, Rich. This is Donna. What can I do for you? spec

M : Ms. Carlson, I'm calling in reference to some suspicious activity on your credit card account. 關於 under spi 可疑的活動 信用卡帳戶 The system detected an unusually large transaction. But first, for your protection, may I have the last four digits of your Social Security number? 偵測到不尋常的大筆交易 基於保護您, 可以要您社會安全碼後四位

W : Sure, 5-5-0-2. Is this about the dining room set I just bought at Wilson's Furniture? 是我購買的餐廳組嗎?

M : Um, yes. Did you make a purchase of $3,294.77 on October 5?

53. (A) Where does the man work?
   - (A) At a bank. 銀行
   - (B) At a furniture store. 傢俱店
   - (C) At a post office. 郵局
   - (D) At a news organization. 新聞組織 (公司)

* complain v.
complaint n. 抱怨. 病痛
Arthritis is a common complaint /ar'θraɪtɪs/ among the elderly.
關節炎
complainant
n. 控訴人. 原告

54. (D) Why is the man contacting the woman?
   - (A) A new credit card will be issued. 新信用卡將被發出
   - (B) A transaction has been reversed. 交易被反轉(撤消了)
   - (C) A delivery was sent to a wrong address. 寄錯地點
   - (D) A large amount was charged to her account. 戶頭被收取一筆大數目

55. (B) What did the woman most likely do?
   - (A) Make a complaint. 提出抱怨
   - (B) Buy some furniture. 買些傢俱
   - (C) Lose her mobile phone. 手機遺失
   - (D) Take out a loan. 借款

complaint
plain
= beat the breast
捶胸悲痛

我們有可以辦大型活動的場地

W : You've been to that fancy Chinese restaurant on Field Street, haven't you? They have facilities for large events, right? I'm in charge of the investor's banquet next month and I need to find a place that could accommodate a group of 50. 要找可以容納50人的地方

M : Yeah, you mean Din Yang Sun. My cousin had his wedding reception in the Mandarin 華語 Room—it's huge, seats 200 people. But I think they have rooms for smaller functions, too.

W : How's the food? (主動)容納;(被動)使就座 Please be seated. 也有適合小集會的房間

M : Great Cantonese-style cuisine. I took some clients from Hong Kong to lunch there a few days ago and they loved it! One guy said it was as good as the food from his hometown! 好吃意 Very authentic. It's pricey, though. Lunch for five was $400 plus service charge.
價格不斐是貴的   5人午餐400美金加服務費   *object

W : That's good to know, but money really isn't an object for this event.
但是錢真的不是這次活動的重點(不用特別省錢) n.目的
宗旨 目標

56. (A) What event are the speakers discussing?
    (A) A banquet. 一場宴會　　　*authentic
    (B) A wedding. 婚禮　　真實的,可信的.真正的
    (C) A business trip. 商務旅行　The report is authentic.
    (D) A client. 客戶　　It's an authentic Van Gogh.

57. (C) What does the man say about the restaurant?
    (A) Service is slow. 服務不好　　revise v.複習,修正,修改了
    (B) The menu needs revision. 菜單需要修改了　see
    (C) The food is very good. 食物很好　revision n.修訂版.校訂.正
    (D) Seating is limited. 坐位有限

58. (D) What does the woman imply? 沒有足夠的時間完成工作
    (A) She doesn't have enough time to finish her work.
    (B) Many employees can't attend the event. 很多員工不能參加活動
    (C) The banquet is not important. 宴會不重要
    (D) Her budget is unlimited. 預算有限

來看我們的室外座位區

Woman US : Satoshi, Louisa from the Gardening Center is here to look at our outdoor seating area. seating plan 座位表 , 露台在餐館的北邊. 沒有太多的直曬陽光

M : Hi, Louisa. The patio's here on the north side of the café, so it doesn't get much direct sunlight. But I'd like to have as many plants as possible to create a comfortable space for our customers to enjoy their coffee. 想要越多植物越好,去創出一個舒服的空間 給客人賞咖啡。

GO ON TO THE NEXT PAGE.

種類 用盆栽裝的植物

Woman UK : Well, there are quite a few species of potted plants that will <u>thrive in</u> that space with indirect sunlight. You should come by the Garden Center tomorrow to see them.

M : Would you mind e-mailing me some photos instead? Some tables are being delivered tomorrow, so I'll need to stay here all day.

59. (B) Where is the conversation taking place?
   (A) At a park.
   (B) At a café.
   (C) At a furniture store. 傢俱店
   (D) At a supermarket. 超商

* thrive in
① 茂盛生長 (長得很好)
⑦ 興旺. 成功 The real estate business is thriving. 房地產蓬勃興隆

* seat 的補充
fly by the seat of one's pants
用直覺放多想
(without a clear plan or direction
→ My parents think that I'm j
flying by the seats of my par
ever since I dropped out of
college

60. (C) What does Louisa suggest that the man do?
   (A) Open a window.
   (B) Use a coupon. 用折價券
   (C) Visit a plant shop. 拜訪植物店
   (D) Extend business hours. 延長營業時間

61. (D) What does the man ask Louisa for?
   (A) A list of prices. 價格明細
   (B) A deadline extension. 期限延長
   (C) Some coffee.
   (D) Some photographs. 一些照片

* extend v. 延長
extension n. 延長

* that reminds me
① 那倒提醒了我
⑦ 我想起來了 → As far as I re
→ If my memory serves m
right
well

Questions 62 through 64 *refer to the following conversation and list.*

發助. 舉辦

M : Hey, Maureen. I'm so excited that GriffCo is <u>sponsoring</u> the 10k run for charity again this corr year. It's a major event with hundreds of participants, so it should be great <u>exposure</u> for us.

W : Oh, <u>that reminds me.</u> Have you looked over this list of <u>graphic design firms</u> we're considering to produce the T-shirts? We need them at least a week in advance of the event, so we have to make a decision soon.

曝光
① 印度神下凡化作人形 ⑦ avatar personality 頭像性格

M : Let me see what you've got there. Hmm. Avatar Studios does some amazing stuff, but our <u>budget has been cut in half</u> from last year's race. 去年比賽起. 預算就減半了

W : You're right. How about these guys in Cleveland? They offer quick <u>turnaround times</u> and their <u>prices are affordable.</u> 負擔得起的價格 (價格合理) 上下貨的來回時間

62. (B) What is the company sponsoring?
   (A) A pancake breakfast.
   (B) A charity run. 慈善路跑
   (C) A golf outing. 高爾夫旅遊
   (D) A <u>weekend retreat</u>. 周末休養所, 周末渡假小屋

go on an outing
excursion
journey

a journey
trip
tour

56

63. (A) What is the man concerned about? 擔心什麼　※ val, vail = strong, worth

(A) A limited budget. 有限的預算
(B) A weather forecast. 氣象預報
(C) A safety issue. 安全問題
(D) An ad campaign. 廣告宣傳

valid adj. 有效的、正確的、健康的
validate v. 確認
validation n. 確認　+test 合格檢查
validity n. 效力, 正當性, 有效性

64. (B) Look at the graphic. Which company do the speakers choose?

(A) Avatar Studios
(B) Buckeye Silk Screen Co.
(C) Icon Design
(D) Taylor & Martin

※ resident

adj 居住的 → a resident student
長駐的

n 居民, 住院醫生

※ medical
adj. 醫療的, 醫藥的
+instrument 儀器
+ condition 病理狀況

Company	Location
Avatar Studios	Columbus
Taylor & Martin	Columbus
Buckeye Silk Screen Co.	Cleveland
Icon Graphic	Cincinnati

剛停在地下室停車庫. 我在想是不是免費提供給洽公民眾。

Questions 65 through 67 refer to the following conversation and building directory.

自動機器

: I just parked in the underground garage and I'm wondering if it's free for visitors on official business. I received this ticket from the automated machine when I entered, but...

: Actually, if you have an appointment with one of our resident medical professionals, I can validate your ticket so you don't have to pay upon exiting. 駐院醫療專業人工 (駐院醫生)

我可以去處理你的票所以出去的時候不用付錢

: That's what I wanted to hear. I have a 4:30 appointment to see Dr. Gupta, but I don't see his name on the building directory. Am I even in the right place?

: Dr. Gupta is the newest addition to the building and just moved in last Friday. So we haven't had time to change the directory. You'll find him in Suite 110.

65. (C) What is the purpose of the woman's visit? 那正是我想聽到的.
但我在樓層介紹上沒看到他的名字

(A) To have her car serviced. 車子被服務
(B) To deliver a package. 送包裹 (維修)
(C) To see a doctor.
(D) To attend a seminar. 參加研討會

→ addition n. 附加物
新成員 ✓
增建物

a new addition of the team
團隊新成員

GO ON TO THE NEXT PAGE.

66. (A) What can the man do for the woman?
(A) Validate her parking. 確認她的停車狀況
(B) Reschedule her appointment. 重新安排她的預約
(C) Park her car. 停她的車
(D) Issue a rain check. 發出改天再約的支票 ① 下次可使用的票根
② 延期改期 Can I take a rain check?

67. (C) Look at the graphic. Which office name has to be updated on the building 表格 directory? 樓層介紹
(A) Unger Fertility Clinic
(B) Kreutz Eye Care
(C) Dr. Karl Edwards, OB-GYN
(D) Smithson Cosmetic Surgery → 整型手術了
化妝品 手術了

DIRECTORY

肥沃; 繁殖力	
Unger Fertility Clinic 診所	Suite 101
Dr. Karl Edwards, OB-GYN	Suite 110
Smithson Cosmetic Surgery	Suite 201
Kreutz Eye Care	Suite 210
Weiner & Associates	Suite 301

Questions 68 through 70 refer to the following conversation and map.
你想點什麼味?
M : Joe's Pizza House, what would you like to order?
W : Hi, Joe. It's Vanessa. I'm on Mill Street by the bus stop right now. I've almost finished delivering the food orders, but this last one doesn't have an address on it.
最後一筆訂單上面沒有地址
M : Hmm, no address. Is there a name?
W : Uh, it's Dan Smith.
讓我查查
M : OK, let me look that up. The Smith order needs to be delivered to the Hazelton Apartment Building, Apartment 12. 在公園正對面
W : Oh, yes, on Durham Road, directly across from the park. Thanks.
/dʒrəm/ /ı'n/

68. (B) Who most likely is the woman?
    (A) A postal worker. 郵件的工作者(郵局工作的人)
    (B) A delivery driver. 送貨員
    (C) A repair technician. 修理工
    (D) A building manager. 建築經理

69. (D) What problem does the woman mention? 提到什麼
    (A) A package has been damaged. 包裹受損
    (B) A vehicle is not working. 車子壞了
    (C) Some residents are not home. 有些居民不在家
    (D) Some information is missing. 有些資訊不見了

70. (D) Look at the graphic. Where will the woman go next?
    接下來要去哪裡
    (A) To building 1.
    (B) To building 2.
    (C) To building 3.
    (D) To building 4.

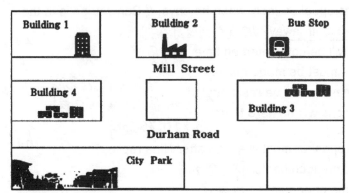

＊ 頻率 adv. 原則上. ① be v. 之後. 一般 v. 之前

I am sometimes wrong.
I sometimes make mistakes.

② 放在 not 之前, always, ever 例外

I sometimes don't make right decisions.
I don't ever make mistakes.
I am not always correct.

✕ 大致的分類

100	always
85	usually
75	frequently
60	often
50	sometimes
40	occasionally
30	rarely
20	seldom
10	hardly ever
0	never

GO ON TO THE NEXT PAGE.

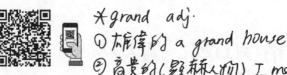

*grand adj.
① 雄偉的 a grand house
② 高貴的(顯赫人物) I met a lot of grand people

Questions 71 through 73 refer to the following telephone message.

要開始請人了

Hi Nina, it's Jeff. We should get started on the hiring process for our new restaurant.

//Can you believe the grand opening is less than a month away?// We have a lot of
有很多履歷要看   你明天有空見面嗎?   如果可以見面的話,
resumes to read through. Are you available to meet tomorrow? If so, I'll e-mail the
我把目前收到的簡歷都寄給你   當我們見面   我們可以比較看
resumes I've received so far. And then, when we meet, we can compare which
          面試哪位候選人
candidates we'd like to interview. Let me know if tomorrow works for you. Thanks.
                                                    is fine with you

71. (A) What is the purpose of the message?   ③ 重大的(獎) I won a grand prize.
    (A) To arrange a meeting. 安排會議
    (B) To confirm an order. 確認訂單   ④ 快樂的 We had a grand holiday.
    (C) To apply for a job. 申請工作   ⑤ 總的 I spent a grand total of
    (D) To make a reservation. 預約.預訂 $150.
                                                                    盛大開幕
72. (B) What does the speaker imply when he says, //"Can you believe the grand opening
    is less than a month away?"//? 只有一個月不到嗎?   *habit 習慣
    (A) Projects will be completed on time. 案子會準時完成   have
    (B) Decisions must be made quickly.   habitual adj.
    (C) Appointments must be rescheduled. → 決定要快點完成   2エ   習慣的
    (D) Reservations will be hard to get. → 會面要重新安排
                                    預約很難取得   habitant 居民
                                                                人
73. (A) What will the speaker most likely do after Nina replies?   habitat 棲息地
    (A) E-mail some documents. 郵寄些文件   2x 2 x
    (B) Make some phone calls. 打電話   cohabit 同居
    (C) Fill out an application. 填寫申請表格   inhabit 居住
    (D) Hire a manager. 雇用經理   inhabitation n.居
                                    inhabitant n.居民

Questions 74 through 76 refer to the following talk.
= To formally begin or restore the orderly functioning of a meeting. inhabitant n.居民
I'll now bring this meeting to order. As you know, we've been working to create a
  徹底的   城鎮郊區
wildlife refuge on the outskirts of town, but unfortunately, we're still lacking the   缺少
必要的資金來進行這個項目
necessary funding to proceed. Now, we've received an offer from a local company to
  豎立   柵欄   沿著   仍然大大的短缺錢錢去建造
erect some fencing along Sunday Creek, but we're still far short of money to construct
          我們應要聯絡這個社區裡的生意人
a bird habitat. I think we should contact some businesses in the community to see if
  2x 2 x   是否願意捐錢
they'd be willing to make a donation. So what I'd like us to do now is draw up a list of
business owners who might be interested in helping with this project. 起草.制定

60 一張老闆名單, 有可能有興趣 幫助這個案子的老闆.

74. (D) What is the talk mainly about?
    (A) Planning an annual celebration. 計畫年度慶祝活動
    (B) Analyzing traffic patterns. 分析起落航線 飛機起落路線
    (C) Attracting visitors to a park. 希別遊客來公園
    (D) Building a wildlife refuge. 蓋一座野生動物庇護所

* refugee 難民
back | flee 逃走

75. (B) What problem does the speaker mention?
    (A) Scheduling conflicts. 行程衝突
    (B) Insufficient funding. 不足夠的資金
    (C) Zoning laws. 分區法
    (D) Broken equipment. 壞掉的設備

`vermifuge n.驅蟲劑
worm

76. (A) What are listeners asked to do? 聽眾被要求?
列出老闆名單(A) Make a list of business owners.
自願做案子(B) Volunteer for a project.
捐錢(C) Donate some money.
選擇-地點(D) Choose a location.

`subterfuge n.藉口
secretly 推託之辭

→ His excuse sounded more like a
subterfuge than a real reason.

Questions 77 through 79 refer to the following advertisement.

是在找(想要買)新的電子設備嗎?   你在想該怎麼處理你的舊電腦,
Are you in the market for a new electronic device? Do you wonder what to do with
卡機   或是其他已沒在使用的電子設備嗎?
your old computers, mobile phones, or other electronic devices you don't use
火車站 倉庫   問題,麻煩
anymore? Well, bring them in to Digital Depot! We'll take the hassle out of recycling
把回收的麻煩拿走 並放些錢在你的口袋   /dɪpo/
your electronic devices and put money in your pocket. When you bring your old
你會收到一張25折的折價券,所有非特價有庫存商品皆
devices to Digital Depot, you'll receive a voucher for 25 percent off any non-sale item
                                                          可用
in stock. To find the Digital Depot location nearest you, visit our website at
www.digitaldepot.com.

*lottery

77. (D) What service is being advertised? 在宣傳/廣告什麼服務
    (A) Computer consulting. 電腦咨詢
    (B) Overnight delivery. 隔夜到貨
    (C) A training course. — 訓練課程
    (D) A recycling program. 回收方案.活動

① 運氣: Life is a lottery.
② 票透彩: win the lottery
He won a million dollars in the
                              lottery.

78. (C) How can listeners receive a discount?
    (A) By completing a survey.
    (B) By visiting the website.
    (C) By recycling an electronic device.
    (D) By entering a lottery. 參加票透活動

買彩透 → buy the lottery ✗
buy the lottery ticket
scratch-off
lottery ticket

GO ON TO THE NEXT PAGE

79. (D) What does the speaker say can be found on a website?
    (A) Recycling information.
    (B) Discount vouchers.
    (C) Instructional videos.
    (D) Store locations.

[handwritten notes: 連 because, for, as, since 放句首時要逗點. 不和 so 連用 「比較」 I am willing to do anything for you because I love you. (連) because of love (介)]

Questions 80 through 82 refer to the following announcement.

Attention passengers traveling on Triad Air Flight 7G434 to San Antonio. <u>Due to</u> mechanical issues, the flight has been canceled. We apologize for the inconvenience, and request that all passengers proceed to the Triad Air customer service desk in the main concourse. An airline representative will book you on a different flight and onward to your final destination. While you're waiting, Triad Air representatives will provide you with complimentary <u>snacks and drinks</u>. Again, we regret the inconvenience and thank you for flying with Triad Air.

*[handwritten notes: refreshments; (介)之 (you can fly / travel); *due to = on account of = thanks to = owing to = in consequence of = by virtue of = by reason of = as the result of = because of; *appreciate v. 感謝.喜歡.欣賞]*

80. (B) Where is the announcement being made?
    (A) At a shopping mall.
    (B) At an airport.
    (C) At a bus terminal.
    (D) At a train station.

81. (B) What does the speaker ask listeners to do?
    (A) Return at a later time.
    (B) Go to the customer service desk.
    (C) Apply for a refund.
    (D) Contact another airline.

82. (D) According to the speaker, what will be <u>distributed</u>?
    (A) Headphones.
    (B) Reading materials.
    (C) Hotel vouchers.
    (D) Refreshments.

Questions 83 through 85 refer to the following talk.

Guys, if you don't mind, I'd like to get started. Today, we'll be reviewing the latest customer survey results for our new bread maker, the Noxa 350. As you're all aware, the bread maker includes a lot of great new features. And our customers <u>appreciate</u>

62

the upgrades. According to the survey, the most popular feature of the bread maker is the diamond-coated pan and kneading blade, which are scratchproof and easier to clean than our last model. But because of all the added features, //the user's manual is currently about 10 pages too long//. So, the editors will be working on that this week.

83. (C) What is the main topic of the meeting?
    (A) A competitor's products.
    (B) An instructional video.
    (C) Survey results.
    (D) An online review.

84. (D) What feature of the product does the speaker mention?
    (A) Remote control.
    (B) Color options.
    (C) Durability.
    (D) Easier cleaning.

85. (B) What does the speaker imply when he says, //"the user's manual is currently about 10 pages too long"//?
    (A) Pages will be added to the manual.
    (B) The manual will be shortened.
    (C) The manual is available to download online.
    (D) Customers should read the manual thoroughly.

Questions 86 through 88 refer to the following announcement.

Welcome, folks. We're happy to see all of you here at People Power Staffing agency today. As you may know, People Power specializes in the placement of employees in temporary and long-term positions across a wide range of industries from advertising to transportation. As time allows, you'll meet individually with our recruiting specialists who have the experience to match your skills with the needs of our client companies. Obviously, we have standing-room only here in this waiting room, so please be patient and the next available specialist will be with you. Now, to help speed up the process, I'd like everybody to make a copy of your photo ID. The copy machine is right over here.

GO ON TO THE NEXT PAGE.

86. (A) What type of business does the speaker work for? *advertise — advertisement
   (A) An employment agency. 人力公司　v.為 ~做廣告　n.廣告.宣傳
   (B) A fitness center. 健身中心
   (C) An advertising firm. 廣告公司　/advertiser
   (D) A shipping company. 貨運公司　n.廣告客戶

87. (D) What does the speaker imply by, //"standing-room only"//?
   (A) He is pointing out that the office will close soon. 指出說新公室很快關門
   (B) He recommends that(a project date be extended. 他建議延遲某了的日期
   (C) Some seats are still available. 有些座位還有
   (D) The room is very crowded. 房間很擁擠　*brokerage

88. (A) What does the speaker ask the listeners to do? n.仲經濟業.經紀業務
   (A) Make a copy of their identification. 複印 ID　佣金
   (B) Complete some paperwork. 文書作業完成
   (C) Stand at attention. 腳跟靠手臂直站好
   (D) Confirm their contact information. 確確他們的聯絡資訊

Questions 89 through 91 *refer to the following talk.*

股票經濟公司. 證券行

Great to see everybody this morning. I hope your internship in our <u>brokerage firm</u> has

been a good experience for you so far. Today, I want you to help us promote the
即將到來的投資研討會　　課程　　包含　一場演說　避險基金經理
upcoming <u>investment seminar</u>. The program will include a talk by hedge fund manager
　　　　　　　　　　　　　　　　　　拿至少100張傳單
Mark Greenfield. So, I'd like each of you to take at least 100 flyers with you today and
發送
distribute them around the building. In addition to handing them out to <u>brokers,</u> you'll

be visiting some of the local businesses in the area. Don't worry. I'll give you a map
我把要給入們去的地方圈起來　　　請不要晚於 3:00 回到辦公室
where I circled the places I want you to go. Please be back at the office no later then

3:00 p.m. Have a great day!

88 (C)
89. (A) Where do the listeners work?
   (A) At a brokerage firm.　stand at attention 股票證券經濟人
   (B) At an art gallery. 藝廊　　stand bail for sb./sth.
   (C) At a medical clinic. 醫療診所　①做 ~的擔保人/保釋人
   (D) At a hair salon. 理髮院　　②保證 ~是真實的
   　　　　　　　　　　→ I'll stand bail for that.

90. (C) What will the listeners be doing today?
   (A) Making trades. 做交易
   (B) Attending a seminar. 參加研討會　bail n.保釋(金)(人)
   (C) Distributing flyers. 發送傳單　　v.保釋.幫助脫困
   (D) Watching a film. 看影片　Jimmy bailed me out with economic aid.

=stockbroker

91. (B) What has the speaker done for the listeners?
    (A) Decorated an office. 佈置一個辦公室　decorate
    (B) Marked locations on a map. 在地圖上標註地點
    (C) Written recommendation letters. 寫推薦信＝reference
    (D) Provided theater tickets. 提供戲院票　＝ a letter of recommendation

Questions 92 through 94 refer to the following excerpt from a meeting.

身為這家公司的經理，我非常高興來正式的宣佈我們被提名"年度優秀設計獎"

As director of this firm, it gives me tremendous pleasure to formally announce our

nomination for this year's Excellence in Design Award. This is a testament to the hard　這是對於這房間裡

work of everybody in this room. But I specifically want to point out the innovative
多個人認真工作的證明　但我特別提要指出 GS 的創新設計

design by Greg Stiles and his team for the Trenton Tower project. The design was so
和他團隊做的 Trenton Tower 案　這是原創的設計

original that we've received inquiries from competing architectural firms. I'd like to ask
我們收到來自競爭建案公司的詢問　inquiry

Mr. Stiles to talk about what inspired his team to create this remarkable project.
是什麼給他靈感創作出這個非凡的作品　非凡的.卓越的

92. (D) What kind of business does the speaker work for?
    (A) A local jeweler. 當地珠寶商　＊ˊarchitect n.建築師
    (B) A public relations agency. 公關機構　chief builder
    (C) A department store. 百貨公司　ˊarchitecture
    (D) An architectural firm. 建築公司

93. (D) What is the speaker announcing? 說話者宣佈什麼　n.建築學.建築風格
    (A) A new partnership. 新的合夥夥伴 (合作案)
    (B) A groundbreaking ceremony. 破土典禮　＊nominate v.提名.任命.
    (C) An employee promotion. 職員晉升　name　指派
    (D) An award nomination. 獎項提名　ˊnominal adj.名義上的
                                          →He is the nominal chairman.

94. (C) What does the speaker say about Greg Stiles's project?
    (A) It promoted collaboration across departments. →提升了跨部門合作
    (B) It led to changes to a company policy. →導到公司政策的改變
    (C) It attracted interest from competing firms. →吸引到競爭公司的興趣 (引起)
    (D) It made use of eco-friendly materials.
        make use of 利用環保素材

Questions 95 through 97 refer to the following recorded message and order form.

Hi, this is Rachel Gretz from Village Supply. I'm calling for Hank Brady. Hank, I've just
我看了你最近的訂單，我想要跟進你訂的 Post-it notes 的數量
had a look at your most recent order and I wanted to follow up on the number of Post-It

notes you've ordered. It seemed unusual that you'd want ten times the normal amount,
看起來不太尋常.你要了一般量的10倍

GO ON TO THE NEXT PAGE.

so I went ahead and adjusted the number to match your regular order. Call me back
if the number was intentional. By the way, I'll be out of the office next week, so Terry
Finch will be handling my accounts while I'm gone. Give him a call at 877-0909
extension 34 if you have any issues.

*go ahead 下
放意的、有意的
我下週不在辦公室
趁我不在的時候
若有任何問題請撥877-0909分機34*

95. (D) Look at the graphic. Which quantity on the order form will be changed?
   (A) 2.
   (B) 4.
   (C) 10.
   (D) 200.

*n.圖表   n.量
adj.生動的、鮮豔的、圖解的
哪一個訂單量會被改變?*

*go ahead
①前進: You go ahead and I'm coming.
②發生: The construction of the bridge will go ahead as planned.
③取得速度 → He is going ahead fast.*

ORDER FORM	
Item	**Quantity**
Inkjet cartridges (B&W)	10
Time cards (50 ct.)	2
Post-It notes (100 ct.)	200
Coffee filters (10 ct.)	4

→太多了 不合理

96. (A) What did the speaker say she did?
   (A) Adjusted the quantity of an order. 調整訂單的量
   (B) Gave a product demonstration. 商品展示
   (C) Inspected a facility. 檢查設備
   (D) Went on vacation. 去渡假

*adjust /ə'dʒʌst/ v.6調整 改變,以適應
inspect v.檢查;檢閱*

97. (B) What does the speaker say about Terry Finch?
   (A) He will be training a new employee. 訓練新員工
   (B) He will be taking care of some accounts. 照顧一些客戶 (處理)
   (C) He will deliver the shipment. 送貨
   (D) He will maintain the website. 維護網頁

***Questions 98 through 100** refer to an excerpt from a meeting and neighborhood map.*

大家請注意
我們在MV區的所有餐廳生意都很好

OK, guys, if I could have your attention, please. Business has been great at every one
of our restaurant locations in Moreland Valley. And we've received a lot of inquiries

我們也收到很多關於外送食物
的詢問
由於 我們從來沒有提供過外送服務,我又想之在一個地點

about food delivery. Since we've never offered delivery before, I'd like to try it at just

試做
雖然 Lakeview餐廳是最市中心的

one location first. Although our Lakeview restaurant is the most central, I think it's best

we start in the smallest neighborhood because that's the most residential location.

我覺得我們應該在最小的鄰近區開始,因為那是最多住宅的區域

66

Plus, we've gotten a lot of requests from that area. We need to get the word out
~~而且~~ 我們收到很多來自那個區域的需求 我們要讓那裡居來的聲音被聽見
though, so let's take some time now to discuss how we can advertise this new service.
我們花些時間來討論如何宣傳,行銷這分新服務.

98. (A) What type of business does the speaker own?
- (A) A chain of restaurants. 餐廳連鎖店
- (B) A flower shop. 花店
- (C) A taxi service.
- (D) A local grocery store. 當地雜貨店

99. (A) Look at the graphic. In which neighborhood does the speaker want to offer a new service?
- (A) North Park.
- (B) Lakeview.
- (C) Arlington Heights.
- (D) South Valley.

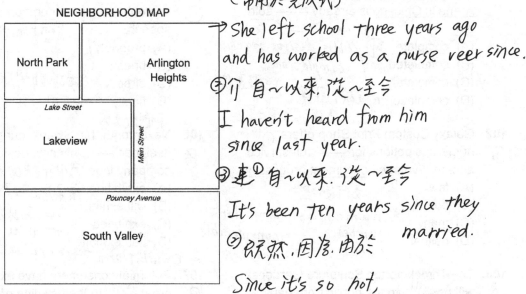

NEIGHBORHOOD MAP

North Park
Arlington Heights
Lake Street
Lakeview
Main Street
Pouncey Avenue
South Valley

★ since
①. adv. 此後. 以前. 從那時到現在
(常用於完成式)
→ She left school three years ago
and has worked as a nurse ever since.
② 介 自~以來. 從~至今
I haven't heard from him
since last year.
③ 連① 自~以來. 從~至今
It's been ten years since they
married.
② 既然.因為.由於
Since it's so hot,
let's go swimming.

100. (C) What does the speaker want to discuss next?
- (A) An updated vacation policy. 新版的休假政策
- (B) A renovation project. 輕修柔
- (C) Advertising strategies. 廣告策略
- (D) Hiring procedures.
顧用流程

GO ON TO THE NEXT PAGE.

*complete He demanded complete silence.
adj. 完整的;附帶的 He bought a house complete with furniture.

In the Reading test, you will read a variety of texts and answer several different types of reading comprehension questions. The entire Reading test will last 75 minutes. There are three parts, and directions are given for each part. You are encouraged to answer as many questions as possible within the time allowed. → v. 完成: complete the work

You must mark your answers on the separate answer sheet. Do not write your answers in your test book.

*attention n. 注意;專心;照顧
to have one's attention 引起/得到/維持 某人的注意力
get / hold
to give sb one's full attention 給予某人某人的全部注意力

PART 5

Directions: A word or phrase is missing in each of the sentences below. Four answer choices are given below each sentence. Select the best answer to complete the sentence. Then mark the letter (A), (B), (C), or (D) on your answer sheet.

for the duration of the meeting 開會的期間

---

101. The summer concert series at Marshall Arena in Chicago is already sold out.
(A) complete (up)
(B) completed
(C) completely ✓
(D) completion n. 完成;圓滿

His desires reached completion.
心願達成
做很多的選擇

102. Galaxy Custom Print Shop offers numerous options for ------- full-service and do-it-yourself document processing.
(A) few
(B) both
(C) many
(D) neither

文件處理
* numerous = abundant
number = considerable
count = various

103. The Throckmorton Sculpture Gardens will be ------- to the public from early spring to late autumn.
(A) open
(B) grown
(C) noticed
(D) entered

介係詞;形容詞
從早看到晚秋
*produce 農品
produce
incorporated v. 製造;引起

104. Spokane House Plans Inc. is looking for an ------- to coordinate multi-family housing projects.
(A) architecture
(B) architecturally
(C) architectural adj. 建築的
(D) architect

找建築師來合作家庭的房屋案
chief builder n. 建築師

105. Be sure to speak ------- into the microphone for the duration of your speech.
(A) probably
(B) briefly
(C) directly
(D) finally

directly adv.
hard / last n. 持續
持續時間
演講期間請直接對
麥克風說話 / 務記有
下個月(未來)

106. Next month, Mr. Swank, our graphic designer, ------- his new designs for the company logo.
(A) exhibiting
(B) will exhibit
(C) exhibited
(D) has exhibited

我們的平面設計師會
展示公司設計的新logo
exhibit v. 展示
out / have
exhibition n. 博覽會 /ɪgˈzɪbɪt/ 展現

107. Potential consumers have expressed great ------- in the new line of trucks from Rodeo Motors.
(A) benefit 好處
(B) interest 利息;興趣
(C) attention 注意力
(D) advantage 優點

對於新的卡車系列
表現出高度興趣 (up)

108. Survey results show that a ------- of consumers would like a wider variety of locally-sourced and organic produce.
(A) point 點
(B) complaint 抱怨
(C) majority 大多數
(D) summary 概要

調查結果顯示大部分的消費者
喜歡更廣泛種類的當地
種植和有機農產品

14

109. Construction will not begin on the new escalator near the Houston Street subway entrance _____ next week.
(A) behind
(B) since
(C) until
(D) in

[handwritten] C / 靠近HS地鐵入口的手扶梯 / 工程直到才通搖開始。 / not until 直到~才~ / 同位語 established 已建立的 / start up company 新創公司

110. First Data Corporation, an Atlanta-based company, assists its new employees with relocation expenses.
(A) established
(B) establish
(C) establishing
(D) establishes

[handwritten] A / 協助員工搬家開支 / 現在分詞=進行.持續·主動 / 過去分詞=完成.被動

111. After _____ reviewed the documents, please sign the approval form
(A) you've
(B) your
(C) yours
(D) yourself

[handwritten] A / have + Vpp / 你看完文件後請簽同意表格 / 提供大方的假期時間 (提供多假期)

112. _____ employee benefits, Chasen-Hoff Biometrics offers a generous amount of vacation time.
(A) For example
(B) In terms of
(C) Because
(D) Whereas

[handwritten] B / measure / 生物統計學 / *bid n.出價.投標 / 就~方面而言 / Our firm won the bid. / make a bid for sth 投標 / 得標

113. The town of Downers Grove is _____ bids from local companies to build a new picnic area at Maple Lake Park.
(A) proceeding
(B) competing
(C) electing
(D) accepting

[handwritten] 可以接受當地公司投標建造新的野餐區域 / proceed(不) / ①繼續進行 / ②著手·開始做 / The project is proceeding as planned. / 擇愛

114. Although the research project has been approved, it is still not _____ clear how will be funded.
(A) perfected
(B) perfect
(C) perfectly
(D) perfection

[handwritten] proceed from 出自 / The whole trouble proceeded from a misunderstanding. / adv. / n.

115. Smoking, eating and drinking are _____ forbidden in the theater.
(A) strict
(B) strictly
(C) strictest
(D) stricter

[handwritten] adv. / B / *forbid v.禁止,不許 / The new law forbids smoking in offices. / *strict adj.嚴格的

116. _____ of the construction work on the Hamilton Skyway will be performed at night to minimize the traffic congestion.
(A) Already
(B) Usually
(C) Most
(D) Almost

[handwritten] C / adv. / 大部分的工程作業會在晚上進行,以最小化交通阻塞的情形 / *refrain / back fract, frag=break

117. Visitors must refrain _____ using flash photography inside the museum's French impressionism exhibit.
(A) with
(B) among
(C) through
(D) from

[handwritten] D / from v.禁止 / 主義,學說,特性 / communism 共產主義 / capitalism 資本主義 / pessimism 悲觀主義 / optimism 樂觀主義 / 遵守

118. Failure to comply with the rules _____ on this list will result in the loss of computer lab privileges.
(A) outlined
(B) outlines
(C) outlining
(D) outline

[handwritten] A / 不遵守名單上的條款會導致失去使用電腦室的權利 / 特權恩典.殊榮 / It's a great privilege to know you.

119. Fulcrum International Holdings has agreed to buy Vandersloot Logistics in a deal _____ up to two billion dollars.
(A) except
(B) together with
(C) worth
(D) on account of

[handwritten] C / which is worth up to / being / 因為

120. Ms. Bettencourt has requested that _____ related to the upcoming relocation be reported separately.
(A) expenses
(B) expensively
(C) expensive
(D) expensed

[handwritten] A / B小姐要求和即將到來的搬家支出要分開報告 / expense n.支出.費用 / at sb's expense 由某人付 / at public expense 公費支出

GO ON TO THE NEXT PAGE

121. Due to hazardous weather conditions, the outdoor dinner to benefit Pine Ridge Children's hospital has been ------- until August 3.

(A) programmed
(B) defined
(C) classified
(D) postponed

由於危險的(不好的)天氣狀況，有鑑於PRC醫院的戶外晚餐已經被延到8月3號
分類的、機密的
define 下定義 defined adj. 清晰的

122. Ascott CEO Carly Kittson claimed that creating the partnership with Morton Manufacturing is her ------- accomplishment.

(A) gratify
(B) more gratified
(C) most gratifying
(D) gratifyingly

CEO說和MM詞建立夥伴關係(合夥)是她最滿意的成就 gratify v.使滿意
please make 滿意
gratitude n. 感恩之情
gratification n. 滿足、令人滿意之事

123. Road Rage Automotive is a trusted brand with a ------- for developing innovative products and supporting them with outstanding customer service.

(A) confirmation
(B) caption
(C) reputation
(D) recognition

值得讓信賴的品牌
研發創新商品
確認、批准
字幕、標題
傑出的客服 recognize v. 認出
名聲
認出、承認、認可

124. As managing editor, Elizabeth Hankey ensures that technical manuals are written in plain language that the general public can understand.

(A) plain
(B) plainest
(C) plainly
(D) plainness

身兼總編輯
*她確保技術手冊(說明書)是用淺顯易懂的語言寫意的，這樣普羅大眾才能看得懂 *plain adj.*
簡樸的、一般的、清楚的、平易的

125. ------- nutritional information for our energy drinks is available on our website.

(A) Detailing
(B) Detailed
(C) Detail
(D) Details

n. 小裝飾品
adj. 詳細的
n. 細節
I must be plain with you.

126. Dennis Everton, service manager of Northwest Car Center, is overseeing ------- with auto-glass suppliers in the Brookfield area.

(A) negotiate
(B) negotiates
(C) negotiations
(D) negotiated

DE, NCC的服務經理主管跟B區域汽車玻璃供應商的協商。
* *oversee 監督、管理*
析的

127. Consumer advocates in Saudi Arabia have ------- concern about proposed Internet regulations.

(A) focused
(B) appeared
(C) applied
(D) expressed

提倡者、擁護者
著重 致力於保護、促進
展現 消費者權益的人
應用的
表達

128. ------- other year, Johnson Motors Inc., conducts a customer-satisfaction survey to determine how warranty services can be improved.

(A) During
(B) Only
(C) About
(D) Every

每隔一年=每兩年
執行客戶滿意度調查，來決定保固服務如何改進
conduct v. 執行
determine v. 決定

129. Live seafood such as lobsters and crabs must be shipped in a ------- that does not expose them to extreme temperatures.

(A) type
(B) behavior
(C) manner
(D) purpose

龍蝦 螃蟹
*活的海鮮一定要用不會使牠們暴露在極端溫度中的方法運送 *manner*
方法、禮貌、規矩

130. Lee Yuan Mining Group is expected to ------- the planned expansion of its rare earths excavation in Kenya during the press briefing on Wednesday.

(A) announce
(B) organize
(C) reflect
(D) suppose

新聞發佈會
excavation n.
excavate v. 挖
/ˈɛkskəˌvet/ (洞、古物)
out hollow
反射
應該
(A)宣佈 (B)組織

Directions: Read the texts that follow. A word, phrase, or sentence is missing in parts of each text. Four answer choices are given below each of the texts. Select the best answer to complete the text. Then mark the letter (A), (B), (C), or (D) on your answer sheet.

Questions 131-134 refer to the following e-mail.

To: Trent Hong

From: Veronica Carson

Date: May 4

Subject: Monroe City

Dear Trent,

I was recently informed of your upcoming ------- to the Monroe City office. As you ------- for the big move, I want to wish you the best and offer my
131.   132.
assistance. I'm familiar with the ------- you'll face during the transition.
133.
So don't hesitate to contact me if you need any help.

134.

Best wishes,
Veronica Carson

[handwritten notes: ✱transition 轉變、過渡期 / It's in a state of transition. 處於轉變期 / V + Ving are preparing 所有格 + N. / conj. 當…的時候 prepare V. / adj. / 積欠、休假利並提後協助 / +N. 我很清楚、熟悉你在這轉變過程中會過到的挑戰 / 別猶豫請聯繫找若你 需要任何幫助]

131. (A) award 獎項
(B) introduction 介紹
(C) transfer 移交、遷移
(D) event 事件

132. (A) prepare ✓
(B) prepared Ved
(C) preparing V-ing
(D) have prepared have Vpp

133. (A) challenging V-ing
(B) challenged Ved
(C) challenger 挑戰者
(D) challenges 挑戰 N.

134. (A) What's more, the Monroe City office is larger and has more parking
(B) Otherwise, the management team is considering your proposal
(C) In the meantime, I have no doubt that you will succeed in your new role
(D) Nevertheless, I have chosen to accept this relocation

[handwritten notes: (B) 除此之外, 管理團隊在考慮你的提案 / (c) 與此同時, 我一點都不懷疑你在你的新角上會成功. (你一定會成功) / ✱doubt n. v. 懷疑. 不相信 / 而且, 更有甚者, 新辦公室大更多停車空間 / (D) 不過, 我已經選擇接受這次搬遷 / nevertheless adv. 不過. 仍然, 依然, 盡管如此 conj. 不過, 然而 / → We are going nevertheless we shall return. 我們要走了, 不過我們還要回來]

GO ON TO THE NEXT PAGE.

17

138 (A) 項在，其他有名的餐廳在考慮 類似的政策改變，在接下來月份裡。

(B) 給小費的其中一個大問題是，明顯的不公平。一個聰明的服務生，會費出辦法來躲避這個系統呢呃

Top Restaurant Shakes Up the Industry

adj. 有名的　　小飯館　　服務生

SONOMA — Renowned eatery El Dorado Kitchen is making

這上全國頭條　　實施 不給小費政策　　生效

national ------- by putting a 'no tipping' policy in effect. The

135.

throughout 場所，上班地點

restaurant has 'No Tipping' signs posted ------- its facility, and

136.

當顧客用信脹付款，上面沒有留小費的　選項在訂餐收據上。

when customers pay by credit card, there is no option to

leave a tip on the order receipt. The restaurant's research

餐廳研究顯示

說超過80%的都喜歡這個政策　　因為

showed that over 80% of customers like the policy because it

用餐最後不用算數學

takes away the need for math at the end of a _meal_. Owner

老闆 和 廚師長在面談中揭露說 收到如潮水般的正面評論

137

and head chef Bob Conway revealed in an interview that he's

been inundated with positive reviews. -------.

138.

into
onto wave 潮水般的(湧來．充滿．壓例) → The village was inundated by

→ I was inundated with work tsu

recently.

＊monument → monumental → a monumental achievement
advise adj. 紀念碑的
remind 不朽的
n. 紀念碑，紀念館，遺物 巨大的

135. (A) monuments
D (B) footnotes 註腳，補充說明
     (C) titles 標題
     (D) headlines 報紙大標，單篇標

136. (A) among → subtitle 副標，字露
B (B) throughout 遍佈，賈穿，從頭到尾
     (C) above 在～之上，勝過
     (D) upon 刪除

在～之上　(C) The moon is above the trees.

137. (A) ride
B (B) meal
     (C) rehearsal 排演 Tim ranks above Tom.
     (D) complaint n. (D) He laid a hand upon my shoulder.
         complain v.

138. (A) Now, other popular restaurants in the area
A are considering a similar policy change in the upcoming months
     (B) One of the big problems with tipping is that it's obviously unfair, and smart servers have figured out how to cheat the system 抽花稅
     (C) Restaurants give up a significant tax credit by eliminating tips, and the potential effect on menu prices is uncertain 對菜單的可能影响未
     (D) A recent study indicates cutting tips could actually hurt servers, and El Dorado has significantly scaled back its trial run
         相當程度地　縮小，減少　試做

最近的研究顯示減少小費 會傷害到服務品質

Annette Shapiris
9900 Ventura Boulevard
Sherman Oaks, CA 90031

Dear Ms. Shapiris,

Your records _____ that you have dental conditions that are still untreated.
139.

During your dental exam on April 12, these problems were noted:

- Decay on teeth #3, 14, 15, 31
- Abscess on tooth #31

- Broken tooth #19
- Gum disease

_____.
140.

Please contact us to schedule your appointments to treat these dental problems before they progress _____. We are happy to review your treatment plan if you
141.
would like. If it has been more than three months since your exam, you might need a new exam in order to reevaluate your problems and update your _____ treatment.
142.

Sincerely,
Farquar Niles & Associates, DDS

139.
(A) process
(B) indicate
(C) explain
(D) examine

140.
(A) The schedule fills up quicker as the end of the year approaches
(B) Your tooth has been prepared for a new crown
(C) We will gladly return the enclosed authorization with their name and address
(D) Delaying treatment of these problems will only result in further damage

141.
(A) farther
(B) further
(C) furthest
(D) furthermore

142.
(A) apprehensive
(B) recommended
(C) complimentary
(D) unusual

GO ON TO THE NEXT PAGE.

核心 = Full employment is the axis of their campaign.

植物(主藝)

Infoaxis, an IT solutions and ------- company, has announced an
143. service　宣佈了公司搬家和擴展

office relocation and **expansion**. The New Jersey-based firm

has moved its offices from Allendale to downtown Newark. The

move stems from Infoaxis' need for ------- space to accommodate
144. additional　開發更多的空間來容納
對公司服務的需求成長

growth in demand for the firm's services. The company has
公司這次搬家室內面積動

more than doubled its square footage with the move. -------.
145. 大兩倍　室內面積

我們看到這幾年的快速成長，
公司新地點和新辦公室

"We have seen our growth accelerate over recent years, and our
to quick　以加速.促進

new location and facilities will allow us to continue **enhancing**
會讓我們持續加強　加強

our ability to serve our customers ---at--- the highest levels," says
146. 我們的能力.用最高階方式來服務客戶

Infoaxis' co-founder and President Gabi Haberfeld.
新的辦公處心有高科技公司簡報室和最先進的.資料中心

The new facility is equipped with a high-tech corporate briefing

room and a new **state-of-the-art** Data Center.
最先進的.高科技的
145 (A)未偵查到的錯誤是
低可靠度和飛機線路高維修
的主要原因。

145 (B) 有大量的存在 (點多.員工多)
整個洲有將近5千名員工。

143. (A) services 服務
A　(B) location 地點
　　(C) partner 夥伴
　　(D) exercise 運動

144. (A) additional 附加的.多的.額外的
A　(B) optional 選擇的 (非必需的)
　　(C) conditional 有條件的，以~為條件
　　(D) seasonal 季節的　的
　　　　　週期性的

145. (A) Undetected faults are the primary contributor
C　　to low reliability and high maintenance in
　　　aircraft wiring 低信賴度　維修
　　(B) Infoaxis has a significant presence in
　　　Massachusetts, with nearly 5,000 employees
　　　across the state　大規模的
　　(C) At 14,000 square feet, the building gives
　　　Infoaxis the opportunity for massive expansion
　　(D) Since 1999, Infoaxis has helped business
　　　owners get a real return on their technology
　　　investments 幫助老闆們在科技投資上得到
　　　　　真正的回報

146. (A) in
D　(B) for　(C)有14,000 坪，這棟大樓給 Infoaxis
　　(C) of　　大擴展的機會。
　　(D) at

irections: In this part you will read a selection of texts, such as magazine and newspaper articles,
mails, and instant messages. Each text or set of texts is followed by several questions. Select the
est answer for each question and mark the letter (A), (B), (C), or (D) on your answer sheet.

estions 147-148 refer to the following notice.

PUBLIC NOTICE

The Huntsville Ombudsman is holding its annual Huntsville Metro
Recycling Day on Saturday, August 31, between 8:00 a.m. and
6:00 p.m. at Juanita Castro Park. This is an opportunity for local
residents to dispose of items they no longer use, including
appliances, furniture, and electronic devices such as computer
equipment. Items will be sold in a community sale or recycled when
possible. Please make sure that personal information has been
deleted from donated electronic equipment. All proceeds from the
sale of donated items support the "Keep Huntsville Clean" project.
Don't miss the opportunity to do some spring cleaning and help our
local environment.

Do you want to donate something that won't fit in your car? We will
be happy to send a truck to pick it up for you. Call D'Andre Flint at
909-5126 to make arrangements. Volunteers are needed to help
sort donations. To volunteer, call Niko Variakis at 909-5122.

---

7. What are Huntsville residents asked to
do?
(A) Review a local recycling policy.
(B) Update their computer equipment.
(C) Donate unwanted items.
(D) Provide personal information.

148. Why should residents call Mr. Flint?
(A) To volunteer to drive a truck.
(B) To subscribe to the Huntsville
Ombudsman.
(C) To make reservations at Juanita
Castro Park.
(D) To request help transporting an
item.

GO ON TO THE NEXT PAGE.

To: Kim Shelby

From: North Pacific Airlines Passenger Services

Time/Date: April 15, 12:40 P.M.

訊息通知　　　　看下面的行程更改

MESSAGE ALERT: See below for schedule 149
changes for North Pacific Airlines Flight 7G600

Flight 7G600 Osaka International Airport (ITM) to 150
Taoyuan (Taiwan) International Airport (TPE)

DELAYED 延遲

Scheduled departure 4:15 P.M. 預計出發

Actual departure 5:30 P.M. 實際出發

Estimated arrival at TPE: 8:15 P.M. 預計到達

Departure gate: To be announced

Baggage claim: Carousel 4 轉盤4號 (baggage carousel)

行李領取　　　　kærəe

If you have a connecting flight, please check with
our ground service crew for transfer information.

如果你需要轉機.

請和我們的地勤人員確認
轉機資訊。

---

149. Why was the text message sent?

(A) To inform a passenger of a cancellation. 通知旅客有個取消

(B) To confirm a ticket purchase. 確認買票

(C) To announce a change in flight status. 宣佈飛機狀態改變

(D) To provide an update about lost baggage. 提供遺失包裹的更新狀況

150. What is indicated about Ms. Shelby? 她錯過轉機班機

(A) She missed a connecting flight.

(B) She will depart from Osaka.

(C) She checked two bags onto a flight. 掛2件行程纜

(D) She paid for her flight in Taiwan. 在台灣付機票錢

Questions 151-152 refer to the following information.

replant 改種, 移植

Replanting and Maintenance 維持

When plants are transferred to new locations, special
當植物被轉移到新地點時, 特別的照顧

care is required to ensure that they arrive safely and
是需要的, 來確保植物平安的到達

thrive in their new environment. Carry all plants by their
並在他們的環境裡繁盛生長　用植物的容器搬運

containers (or root ball), as carrying them by their tops
或是連植物的根球 起搬. 如果提植物的上面

or trunks may damage the roots. Follow the watering
或者 樹幹, 可能會傷害根部. 並循澆水指示

guidelines in the directions-for-care pamphlet for the
在「照顧方針」小冊子裡

specific type of plant you have purchased. These
你所買的特定品種植物

pamphlets are available free of charge and are located
這些小冊子可以免費取得. 在靠近出口處的櫃台

near the checkout registers.

* pamphlet
= booklet
= brochure

這封資訊主要是給誰的?

151. For whom is the information primarily
intended?
(A) Safety inspectors. 安全檢查員
(B) Store managers. 商店經理
(C) People selling containers. 賣容器的人
(D) People purchasing plants. 賣植物的人

不用錢

152. What is available at no cost?
(A) Boxes. 盒子
(B) Delivery. 運輸
(C) Seed packets. 種子小袋子
(D) Written instructions
寫下的說明

GO ON TO THE NEXT PAGE

Please Join Us!

What: The Sea at Dusk: The world-premiere production of noted playwright Oliver Kimball's latest work.

Where: Cavalier Performing Arts Center, Roanoke

When: Saturday, October 12. Bus leaves employee parking area at 9:00 a.m.

Estimated return time: 10:00 P.M.

Cost: $65.00 per person for round-trip transportation, lunch, and admission to the 2:00 p.m. matinee performance. Money will be collected upon boarding the bus During the return trip, we'll make a **brief** stop at the Roanoke Galleria, where you may purchase dinner or a snack if you wish.

Note: To participate, you must sign up in advance on the sign-up sheet in the upstairs break room. The sheet will be **posted** until 5:00 p.m. on October 5. These excursions fill up quickly, so act soon.

For more information, please contact Gabby Susskind at the reception desk (extension 24, or e-mail: gabby@grantland.com)

153. What type of event is being publicized?
- (A) A sightseeing tour.
- (B) A shopping excursion.
- (C) A beach trip.
- (D) A theater outing.

154. Where should participants submit payment for the event?
- (A) At the Cavalier Performing Arts Center.
- (B) In the upstairs break room.
- (C) At the reception desk.
- (D) On the bus.

Planning your next travel experience?
Look no further than Ubertrek International!!

Ubertrek International now offers new vacation packages to an even wider variety of destinations. We have recently partnered with major hotel chains in the world and can offer the best deal in the best locations. New options added for the summer season include:

Sicilian Nights: Spend 6 days and 5 nights on the beautiful Mediterranean Sea aboard the San Giuseppe cruise ship. The ship will dock for special day trips in Palermo, Messina, Syracuse and Marsala.

Grecian Exploration: Tour famous Greek isles. The 10-day, 9-night tour will include visits to Santorini, Argos, Crete, and Mykonos. Package includes airfares, transportation between cities, and hotel stays.

South American Adventure: Explore the wonders of South America on this exclusive 2-week trip. Professor Carlos Enrique, a well-known expert on the history of the region will lead travelers on a tour of the Amazon River and modern Brazil. At the same time, travelers will enjoy the beautiful landscapes, unique culture, and exciting foods of the region. Package include airfares, hotel stays, train fares, and bus transportation.

In addition to these options, Ubertrek continues to offer customers assistance in booking flights and renting automobiles.

155. What has changed at Ubertrek International?
(A) New vacation options have been made.
(B) Additional tour agents have been hired.
(C) Prices on vacation packages have been reduced.
(D) A new office has been opened.

156. Who is Carlos Enrique?
(A) A chef.
(B) A historian.
(C) A landscape designer.
(D) A ship's captain.

157. What is NOT stated about Ubertrek International?
(A) It collaborates with hotel chains.
(B) It helps people reserve rental cars.
(C) It guarantees the lowest rates on air trips.
(D) It offers special options for summer vacation.

GO ON TO THE NEXT PAGE.

Cambridge Medical Associates
67 Edgewater Road
Milwaukee, Wisconsin 65711
September 2

Dear Great Lakes Supply:

In my search for a new supplier, I was referred to your company by a colleague of mine from the Banyan Pharmaceutical Group. He indicated that he has been purchasing supplies from you for more than five years, and after I had mentioned some of the problems I had been having with another vendor, he emphasized your customer service and personable staff.

In fact, I've already found what he said to be true. When I tried to place an order online, I kept getting an error message after clicking the "Submit" button at the end of the form. I telephoned the customer service number, and the representative, Tiffany, explained that there was a temporary problem with the website. Because I was in a rush to get these supplies, she advised me to fax my request instead of mailing it or waiting for the website to come back online. I was surprised by how patiently Tiffany walked me through the steps for finding and printing the order form. I readily completed it and am now sending it as suggested, along with this brief feedback.

Despite initial displeasure over the ordering problem, I was quite pleased by my first interaction with your staff, and I look forward to receiving my first order from your company. Thanks again.

Sincerely,
Consuelo Pineda
Cambridge Medical Associates

158. What is suggested about Great Lakes Supply?
(A) It specializes in selling office machines.
(B) Its customer service representatives request feedback.
(C) Its website has been unavailable for over a week.
(D) It has been in business for at least five years.

159. What is implied about Ms. Pineda's previous supplier?
(A) Its prices were too high.
(B) Its delivery times were unreasonable.
(C) Its website was difficult to use.
(D) Its customer service was poor.

160. How did Ms. Pineda submit her order to Great Lakes Supply?
(A) By postal mail.
(B) By e-mail.
(C) By fax.
(D) By telephone.

From:	Bryant Southern <generalmanager@lacarmela.com.ph>
To:	All staff members <mailing_list@lacarmela.com.ph>
Re:	Employee of the Month
Date:	June 3

Last week, resort owner Hiram Peretz announced his new Employee of the Month program. This program will recognize full-time employees who show an outstanding commitment to serving La Carmela Resort Boracay. Examples of exceptional work include saving the resort money, meeting a difficult deadline, or serving guests in a way that exceeds usual duties.

Nominations may be submitted by any La Carmela Resort Boracay guest or employee. Forms are available at the concierge desk and can also be printed from our website. Nominations for this month are due by June 21. A special box for completed forms has been placed next to the front door. Managers will review the nominations and select the winner during their monthly planning meeting.

La Carmela Resort Boracay employees of the month will receive a monetary award, a certificate of appreciation signed by Mr. Peretz, and an invitation to an annual employee-recognition dinner. We believe that this will be a wonderful opportunity to recognize our hard-working and dedicated employees!

Sincerely,

The Management

161. Where are nomination forms submitted?
(A) By the main entrance.
(B) At the concierge desk.
(C) In the manager's office.
(D) On the hotel website.

162. What is indicated about award recipients?
(A) They have worked at the hotel for at least one year.
(B) They will receive money as part of the award.
(C) They may bring a guest to the employee-recognition dinner.
(D) They will be selected on July 1.

163. What is stated about the resort owner?
(A) He sent the e-mail to everyone in the company.
(B) He will sign certificates of appreciation.
(C) He meets with managers on a monthly basis.
(D) He knows all his employees by name.

GO ON TO THE NEXT PAGE.

Trade Commission Projections Now Available

October 1 — The Edwardsville Trade Commission has released its latest Regional Labor Forecast. – 1 –. The report provides information about the fastest growing industries and occupations as well as those in decline. The report is released biannually, in April and October, to ensure the data reflect the current labor market in Edwardsville and the surrounding region. – 2 –.

Most notably, the greatest job growth is anticipated for teachers, customer service representatives, and registered nurses over the next two quarters. – 3 –. Each of these categories is expected to grow by 5 percent through the remainder of the year. Moderate growth is expected for a majority of positions in the hospitality sector as the tourism industry continues to develop and vacation season begins. – 4 –.

To read the full report, which provides projections for more than twenty industries, visit: www.edwardsville.gov/trade_commission

164. What does the report discuss?
(A) Average local salaries.
(B) Workplace safety concerns.
(C) Future jobs in the area.
(D) Changes in consumer spending.

165. How often is the report published?
(A) Once a year.
(B) Twice a year.
(C) Every month.
(D) Every quarter.

166. The word "over" in paragraph 2, line 2, is closest in meaning to
(A) above.
(B) near.
(C) during.
(D) beyond.

167. In which of the positions marked [1], [2], [3] and [4] does the following sentence best belong?
"However, positions in manufacturing are expected to decline by 10 percent in the greater Edwardsville area."
(A) [1].
(B) [2].
(C) [3].
(D) [4].

Rankin Makes Large Donation to Save Old Springfield

March 30 — Springfield resident and architect Chester Rankin of Parchment Design Group announced yesterday that he is donating one million dollars over the next two years to the Save Old Springfield project. The contribution comes at a critical time, as the project's funding has been declining for the past three years. "We're thrilled to receive Mr. Rankin's generous gift," said Springfield Historical Society (SHS) president Maurice Bovine. "It will go a long way toward conserving the architectural cornerstones of our community."

Save Old Springfield was launched ten years ago by the Springfield Historical Society to restore and preserve buildings from the town's early years. It was originally funded through tax revenue. However, three years ago the town council decided to shift much of that funding away from the RHS and into a new land development initiative. Since then, financial support for the project has remained limited.

Five months ago, SHS began soliciting private donations from larger businesses in the region. "Along with a letter asking for support, we sent photographs of several historic buildings awaiting restoration," Mr. Bovine recalled. One such building was the house on Fordham Street where Chester Rankin grew up. "I didn't know about Mr. Rankin's personal connection to the property until he called me and asked how he could help," Mr. Bovine said. Springfield residents and community leaders have responded enthusiastically to news of the donation. The town council has also suggested putting honorary plaques in several historic landmarks to make the town more appealing to new residents, visitors, and businesses.

Mr. Rankin said in a statement, "When I was a child, I was inspired by the buildings in Springfield. They were instrumental in helping me choose my career. But this gift is not just about preserving the town's history. It's about investing in its future."

— Dieter Neubauer, Beat Reporter

168. When was the Save Old Springfield project started?
(A) Five months ago.
(B) Two years ago.
(C) Ten years ago.
(D) Three years ago.

169. According to the article, why did the project lose funding?
(A) Because the restoration work was completed.
(B) Because construction costs rose unexpectedly.
(C) Because Springfield's population had declined.
(D) Because the local government reduced its financial support.

170. What motivated Mr. Rankin to make the donation?
(A) A personal phone call from Mr. Bovine.
(B) The chance to design historic buildings.
(C) Pictures of his childhood home.
(D) Being chosen to develop new land in Springfield.

171. What does Mr. Rankin suggest about the buildings in Springfield?
(A) They are too expensive to maintain.
(B) They motivated him to become an architect.
(C) Local businesses should pay to restore them.
(D) Each one should have a plaque indicating the year it was built.

GO ON TO THE NEXT PAGE.

29

48-HOUR NOTICE OF INTENT TO ENTER APARTMENT

RESIDENT NAME(S): Davis, Marion

DATE: December 2

PROPERTY: 302 Walker Avenue

APT #: 18A

Dear Resident:

In order to serve you properly, it is necessary to enter your apartment from time to time to perform certain preventive maintenance procedures (such as changing HVAC filters), and to accompany and supervise certain contractors (such as pest control). While we try to make every effort possible to accommodate your schedule, there are times when we must enter your apartment in your absence to ensure continuity of our maintenance program and contracted services.

Your lease gives us the right, upon notification to you, to enter your apartment during normal business hours for the purposes of upkeep, to make repairs and to perform routine inspections. Your lease also provides that, in an emergency, we can enter your apartment without prior notice.

This letter shall serve as our notice to you that we will be entering your apartment on December 5, sometime between the hours of 9:00 a.m. and 5:00 p.m., to perform the following service:

____Pest Control ____HVAC Filter Change ____HVAC Coil Cleaning

  √ Other: **SMOKE DETECTOR MAINTENANCE**

*[Handwritten study annotations present: HVAC = Heating Ventilation Air Conditioning; *absence 缺席 不在場; absence with pay 帶薪休假; *accommodate 便宜納，符合，通融，向~提供; "The policeman accommodate us when we asked for help." "The bank will accommodate him with a loan." and various Chinese glosses throughout.]*

請你確認管理室有所有自從你搬進來後安裝的所有前門 key.

Please make certain that the Management Office has keys to any apartment front door locks you may have installed since moving in. Your lease specifically states that you may not change your locks without the prior written permission of the management, and that you must provide management with a key to any new locks installed. If we are unable to gain entrance to your apartment because of the presence of unauthorized locks, we will be forced to begin eviction proceedings against you.

Please call me should you have any questions. Thank you very much.

Sincerely,

Fred Timmons, Property Manager

cc: Resident File

*proceeding n. 行為. 行動. 事項. 會議記錄

*evict 逐出, 收回(財產)
ex / out | conquer
victor n.
victorious adj. 勝利的
vanquish v. 征服. 擊敗
→ He tried to vanquish his fears.

specifically adv. 特別地 明確地 具體地
/spɪ'sɪfɪk!ɪ/

175 (A) 噴霧殺蟲 (C) 換鎖
(B) 室內抽煙 (D) 室內塗油漆(塗擦)

172. What is this notice mainly about?
(A) Apartment maintenance. 公寓維修
(B) Security guidelines. 安全方針
(C) Guest policies. 賓客政策
(D) Management office hours. 管理室辦公時間

73. What will happen on December 5th?
(A) The elevator won't be in service. 電梯不能用
(B) Marion Davis will go out of town. 不在辦公室
(C) Lobby keys will no longer work. 不能用
(D) The smoke detectors will be tested. 測試煙霧偵測器

174. What might happen if access cannot be gained to Marion Davis's apartment?
(A) A fire could break out. 會發生火災
(B) The smoke detectors will go off. 會感動
(C) She could be evicted. 會被逐出
(D) A locksmith will be called. 會叫鎖匠來

175. What does the lease specifically prohibit without prior written permission?
(A) Spraying for bugs.
(B) Smoking indoors.
(C) Changing the locks.
(D) Painting the interior.

租約明確地禁止沒有事先許可不可以做的事是?

*prohibit v. 禁止. 阻止 不允許
before | have
/pro'hɪbɪt/
→ Smoking is prohibited in many restaurants.
→ Eating after 8:00 is prohibited for those who are on a diet.

prohibition n. 禁止. 禁令
/proə'bɪʃn/

GO ON TO THE NEXT PAGE.

apparently
① 顯然地
② 表面上，似乎
Apparently she did not → succeed.
看樣子她沒有成功。

inform
✓ 通知，報告，告知
② 告發 + against /on
He informed against the drugpusher.
他告發了那個毒販。

To: Greg Espinosa

From: Thad Sayer

Date: Tuesday, January 24

Subject: Phone issue

Dear Greg,

我寫信來討論和我最近搬到7054室的問題

I'm writing to discuss an issue related to my recent move to room 7054.

我已經接下Ash的舊辦公室和電話號碼，由於她已經放了長假

I've taken over Ash Groplus' old office and phone number, as she has

明顯地，客戶並沒有被告知

taken an extended leave from work. Apparently, customers were not

因此 我平均一天收到超過30通

informed about this, and consequently, I have received, on average,

從她客戶打來的電話 這聽起來

over thirty calls a day from her customer accounts. It appears as

員工通訊錄還沒有改好讓他們知道這兩件事

though the employee directory has not yet been changed to let them

① 她不在這兒 ② Mo-Chien此時正處理她的客戶（不是我！）

know that: (A) She is not here; and (B) Mo-Chien Huang is handling

at the same time 必須接這些不是打給我的

her accounts in the meantime. To have to take so many calls that are

電話非常浪費時間和令人分心 有可能

not intended for me is so time-consuming and distracting. Would it be

改一下分機號碼或是連接到我舊分機號 5-7025到7054室嗎?

possible to change the extension number or connect my old extension

number 5-7025 to room 7054? I would greatly appreciate your help.

我會相當感謝您的幫助

Thank you very much.

Thad Sayer

account
n. 帳, 帳目
帳戶
客戶

描述: The policeman gave an account of the traffic accident.

解釋: He gave us a detailed account of his plan.

原因, 理由: He got angry on this account.

STAFF DIRECTORY

Employee name	Ext. number
Garrett Sullivan	5-7079
Ash Gropius	5-7054
Mo-Chien Huang	4-6121
Deidre Kinski	5-7043
Thad Sayer	5-7025
J.T. Carpenter	4-6089
Benny Quayle	5-7065

A "4" prefix designates an office located on the fourth floor

A "5" prefix designates an office located on the fifth floor

176. According to the list, who works on the fourth floor?
(A) Garett Sullivan.
(B) Maria Kinski.
(C) J.T. Carpenter.
(D) Benny Quayle.

177. What is Thad Sayer's current extension number?
(A) 5-7025.
(B) 5-7054.
(C) 5-7065.
(D) 5-7079.

178. In the e-mail, the word "leave" in paragraph 1 in line 3 is closest in meaning to
(A) removal.
(B) absence.
(C) sequence.
(D) departure.

179. What does Thad Sayer say about Mo-Chien Huang?
(A) He has been assigned a certain number of clients.
(B) His employee directory information has not been updated.
(C) He is gathering information for the employee directory.
(D) His technical problems have been resolved.

180. What does Thad Sayer mention in his e-mail?
(A) He has not received a telephone directory.
(B) His office is on the second floor.
(C) He is being unnecessarily interrupted at work.
(D) His telephone isn't functioning properly.

GO ON TO THE NEXT PAGE.

Chris Rossini, Manager

Aldo's Market

374 Lexington Pkwy N

St. Paul, MN 55104

September 27

Dear Mr. Rossini,

Upon reviewing the receipt for my recent purchase at your store, I noticed that I was charged for an extra jar of mayonnaise. I'm certain that I purchased only one jar, but I didn't go back to your store, as I was leaving town for a long weekend the next day. In my haste to get home, I didn't realize the error that day. The cashier I recall was courteous but seemed unfamiliar with your equipment. Since I am one of your longtime satisfied customers, I hope you will agree to correct this error. I would be happy to accept a credit for the same amount toward a future purchase. I have enclosed the receipt of purchase so that you can verify and process the credit, as appropriate. Please contact me at g_blankfeld@lemail if you have any further questions.

Sincerely

Gloria Blankfeld

handwritten annotations:

* haste → More haste, less speed. 欲速則不達。
n. 急忙

* recall v. 回想，使想起，召回

* courteous adj. 殷勤的，謙恭的 /'kɝtjəs/

/meə'nezi/

* satisfied adj. 滿足的，令人滿意的

* verify v. 證明，核對，查資

* process v. 處理，辦理，加工 → processed food 加工食物 n. 過程，進程

* credit n. 賒帳，存款，信用，學分

proceed 列隊前進

34

ALDO'S MARKET
374 Lexington Pkwy N
St. Paul, MN 55104
Thursday, September 21 12:34:09
#AM-29384
Receipt

1 Deli Select Sandwich — PASTRAMI $4.45
1 Deli Select Sandwich — TURKEY $3.85
12 Blueberry muffins   @1.50 $15.00
1 16oz. Gold Star mayonnaise $3.15
1 16oz. Gold Star mayonnaise $3.15
1 Newspaper $1.50

SUBTOTAL $31.00
STATE SALES TAX (8.75%) $2.72

TOTAL $33.72

Cashier   T. Shipp

Thank you for shopping at Aldo's
Open every day 9 AM - 9 PM

1. What most likely caused the problem?
   (A) The cashier's inexperience.
   (B) Ms. Blankfeld's hurry to leave the store.
   (C) Faulty equipment at the store.
   (D) An incorrectly marked price.

2. When did Ms. Blankfeld leave for a trip?
   (A) On September 21.
   (B) On September 22.
   (C) On September 27.
   (D) On September 28.

3. What is NOT on the receipt?
   (A) The cashier's name.
   (B) The manager's name.
   (C) The date and time of the transaction.
   (D) The store's hours.

184. What can be inferred about Ms. Blankfeld?
   (A) She has received good service at the store before.
   (B) She was late for work because of the incident.
   (C) She is moving away from St. Paul.
   (D) She is a good friend of Chris Rossini.

185. What is the purpose of Ms. Blankfeld's letter?
   (A) To place an order for groceries to be delivered.
   (B) To complain about a poorly-made sandwich.
   (C) To suggest a product placement.
   (D) To request a credit for an extra charge.

GO ON TO THE NEXT PAGE

Books by Dick Rivers

visually adv. 視覺上地 直觀地 形象上地

chronicle n. 編年史 把~載入 v. 紀錄

chronic adj. 慢性的 長期的 慣常的

Capture v. 估領 獲得, 捕獲

The Evolution of Music

n. 發展, 演化 音樂的演化

這一切從何開始的呢 Rivers 用眼睛紀錄了整個世紀的音樂演化

Where did it all begin? Rivers visually chronicles the evolution of music through the centuries, from traditional folk music to contemporary dance music. 從傳統的民俗音樂到當代的跳舞音樂

He is a chronic complainer. 他老是抱怨

Look Past the Glass

Rivers 捕捉到一些從洛杉磯到倫敦頂尖音樂家的創作過程

Rivers captures the creative process of some of the top musicians from Los Angeles to London. Spanning almost twenty years, the book is filled with Rivers's photographs and shows what goes on in recording studios before music is released to the masses.

時間橫跨幾乎20年　這本書充滿了　Rivers 的照片 並呈現出 在音樂發佈給大眾之前, 錄音室裡的情況

mass /æ/ 大眾　錄音室

memoir /ˈmemwɑr/ n. 回憶錄 自傳

And The Cradle Will Rock: My Story

懷夢 發源地

一個有趣的, 好玩的回憶錄 關於在音樂和娛樂世界長大。

An amusing memoir about growing up in the music and entertainment world. Rivers writes about his unconventional upbringing in Hollywood with parents who began as touring musicians before launching their own record label.

Rivers 書寫關於 他 非正規的 在好萊塢的成長過程

由他在推出自己專輯前是巡迴歌手的音樂家父母帶大的過程

推出, 發行　唱片專輯　*unconventional* 非慣規的 不依慣例的　*upbringing* 養育, 培育

Revolving Doors: A Decade of Taste

旋轉門

Rivers 這10年間的影象收集 關於流行音樂, 並展示曾經流行什麼, 什麼被認為不酷

A collection of Rivers's images collected throughout a decade of popular music and revealing what was popular, what was considered "uncool", and then what was popular once again after falling out of favor.

然後什麼流行過又不流行　不流行

① 偏好. 喜愛　② 贊成: They will look favor on your proposal.

③ 恩惠: You did me a great favor.

*super food
指對健康非常好，甚至可以對疾病有幫助的食物

CITRUS3
THE INTERNET
RADIO COMPANY

晚間節目，10/3

| HOME | ABOUT | SERVICES | CONTACT |

EVENING PROGRAMMING, OCTOBER 3

6:00 PM — In the Kitchen with Kim
(上)　討論最新的超級食物.是什麼. 提供的好處
Host Kim Pauley talks about the latest super foods; what they are, what they 是什麼
offer, and how best to prepare them. Featured recipes will be available on our 如何準備
website after tonight's show. 好的食譜今晚節目結束後會放在網站上

7:00 PM — Shooting from the Hip　訪談攝影師兼作家Dick關於是什麼促使他
Host Lucy Slate interviews photographer and author Dick Rivers about what
寫他的最新著作　　關於他的童年　他怎麼他的故事
prompted him to write his latest book about his childhood. He shares stories
about what it was like to grow up in the entertainment industry.
關於如何在娛樂業裡長大的事.

8:00 PM — Digital Nation
Host Gary Flax focuses on the latest digital technology. He discusses products
that are really innovative and useful and identifies those that are not.

著重最新科技. 他討論真正創新和實用的商品,並確認那些不是
數位　　　　　　　　　　　　　　　　　　(不是創新和實用的東西)

| Audio Archive | Talent | Sponsors |
檔案文件

*prompt
v. 促使. 激勵. 引起. 激起
揭示. 提詞
adj. 敏捷的. 及時的
He is prompt in paying his rent.

→ He was prompted by patriotism. n. 愛國精神
　　　　　　　　　　ㄞ ㄓˋ ㄓˊ
他被愛國心所激勵

She needed to be prompted three times.
她要別人提示三次

*innovative
adj. 創新的

*identify
v. 確認. 驗明

*entertainment
n. 娛樂. 消遣. 招待
→ We are delighted in entertainment of our friends.
喜歡招待朋友

GO ON TO THE NEXT PAGE.

37

From:	clarisemay@onemail.com
To:	comments@citrus3radio.com
Re:	Dick Rivers/Shooting from the Hip
Date:	October 4

I discovered CITRUS3 Radio over 15 years ago and have been a <u>regular</u> <u>listener</u> of your evening programming for <u>at least</u> a decade. I just wanted to say how much I enjoy your newest program, Shooting from the Hip, hosted by Lucy Slate. I've been interested in many of the authors that have been featured on the show so far, but last evening's guest was especially <u>entertaining.</u> I remember Dick from when he was a little boy. I worked with his parents when they lived in Hollywood, and I <u>recall</u> seeing Dick in his parents' studio most days when most kids were in school. So I was thrilled to learn that he has written about his childhood, and I look forward to reading his new book. Thank you for the excellent programming.

Clarise May

186. What is one <u>common feature</u> in all of Mr. Rivers's books?
(A) They contain personal photographs.
(B) They focus on amateur musicians.
(C) They are set in Hollywood.
(D) They follow events over multiple years.

187. What book did Mr. Rivers discuss on CITRUS3 Radio?
(A) The Evolution of Music
(B) Look Past the Glass
(C) And the Cradle Will Rock: My Story
(D) Revolving Doors: A Decade of Taste

188. What is indicated about Shooting from the Hip?
(A) It is hosted by Kim Pauley.
(B) It was moved to a new time.
(C) It is broadcast every morning at 7:00.
(D) It was recently added to CITRUS3 Radio.

189. In the e-mail, the word "regular" in line 1 is closest in meaning to
(A) frequent.
(B) complete.
(C) curious.
(D) typical.

190. What is probably true about Ms. May?
(A) She was featured on Digital Nation.
(B) She hosts a radio program.
(C) She has worked in the music industry.
(D) She has interviewed Mr. Rivers.

*spin v. ①結網 n. ①兜風: Get your bicycle and coma for a spin.
②放轉 ②(v) 物價暴跌 The news sent prices into a spin.
②(CD) 情緒低落 He has been in a spin since the defeat.
漫遊者 精英 行李箱組合 ①旋轉 to do a spin / perform a spin

https://www.crenshawbush.com/roverelite

CRENSHAW & BUSH

/ˈrovɚ/ /eˈlit/

ROVER ELITE LUGGAGE SET

周末隨身袋 WEEKENDER CARRY-ON	$149
國際直立旋轉 INTERNATIONAL UPRIGHT SPINNER	$349
大型可擴大旋轉 LARGE EXPANDABLE SPINNER	$549

整組了 COMPLETE SET $949 (SAVE 10%)

優雅石板灰 e 即將上市 酷冰銀
COLORS: ELEGANT SLATE (COMING SOON—SILVER ICE)

DETAILS: Are you alone or with a companion? ← *companion [kəmˈpænjən] n. 同伴, 伴侶, 朋友

ROVER ELITE IS A COORDINATED COLLECTION THAT
COMBINES HARD SPINNER CASES WITH SOFT COMPANION
PIECES. TAKE THEM TOGETHER AND GET ROLLING OR
REMOVE ONE AND CONVENIENTLY CARRY IT WITH YOU.

結合 A 硬殼旋轉箱 with B 軟的搭配部分 (兩2件) 一起用或是拿掉一個, 以方便攜帶

為大力使用而設計的
DESIGNED FOR HARD USE, ROVER ELITE IS THE WORLD'S
ONLY CX™ EXPANDABLE HARDSIDE COLLECTION. THE
ROVER ELITE SET FEATURES THREE PIECES THAT ARE BOTH
LIGHTWEIGHT AND DURABLE. 3件物品都很輕並且耐用

- EXPANDABLE CENTRAL POCKETS 可擴大的中間袋子
- OMNI-DIRECTIONAL WHEELS 全方位輪子
- EASY-OPENING, TIGHT-SEALING CLASPS
  好打開, 扣很緊的鉤子, 夾子

GO ON TO THE NEXT PAGE.

*perishable   perish   *´adequate adj.足夠的 ⟷ inadequate
ㄥ ㄧ ㄓ   v.死、腐壞   æ ə ㄑ
adj.易壞的   *relief
   易死的   n.① 緩和、減輕
CRENSHAW & BUSH   ② 慰藉
ROVER ELITE LUGGAGE SET
④ 替換、接替   ③
The relief driver   救濟品：The relief was flown
has got here.   to the flood-hit areas.
替代的司機已經到了   救濟品被空運到洪水氾濫區

Fiona V. Feltham

July 16

我時常出差旅行   時常要帶易壞的樣品在身上 上飛機
I frequently travel for business, often carrying perishable samples
                現代大部分的登機箱都是軟殼的   所以
with me on the plane. Most carry-ons these days are soft-sided, so
      能找到可以提供足夠保護的東西是個解脫(寬心)
it was a relief to find something that offers adequate protection. I've
   我最滿意登機箱
been mostly happy with the carry-on, but the larger bags have
caused some problems. My Elegant Slate spinners look so similar
                                              和其他人的箱子
to everyone else's that other travelers have taken them by mistake 長好多次
on several occasions! More variety would be nice. 拿錯.
好幾次都拿錯.   要有變化會更好,   機械零件
I also have some concerns about the mechanical elements of this
                                                          僵硬的
set. In particular, the retraction mechanism of the handle is stiff and
         æ ə ㄧ   收回機械 (伸縮把手)
frequently gets stuck in the extended position.   收回的那力
常常卡住在延長的狀態(收不回去)

*variety n.變化. People like to live a life full of variety.

* mechanical   * retraction   *in particular
  ə æ ㄧ   n.撤回.收回   尤其是
心. 機械的   特別地
   木板的 無表情的   *mechanism
   細節上的   ㄥ ə ㄧ   * by mistake
   技巧上的   n.機械裝置   錯誤地 (粗心大意)

40

*verify v. 證明.查員.核對   * duplicate n. 副本. 完全一樣的東西

hear about 得知

July 17   You'll hear about this later. 你就等著瞧吧! (一定會被�)

Dear Ms. Feltham,

我們很抱歉得知你的商品問題   我們推出了新顏色選擇了

像你這樣回應的結果 (說另人回應, 就色太力)

We're sorry to <u>hear about</u> your trouble with our product. As a result of feedback like yours, we've introduced a new color option. If you contact us at: support@crenshawbush.com, we'll send you, in our attractive new color, a <u>duplicate</u> of the large expandable spinner to <u>complement</u> your Rover Elite set. <u>Note that</u> this gift will be sent to you after you <u>verify</u> that you posted the July 16 review.

補足

特別注意, 禮物特在你證明你張貼了 7/16 的貼文後寄給你.

We also appreciate your feedback about our luggage <u>components</u>. <u>Rest</u> <u>assured</u> that our handle mechanism has been proven to <u>withstand</u> years' worth of <u>rough treatment</u>, retracting and extending smoothly over 10,000 times under stressful conditions in our laboratories.

保證   低擋

很舊的對待 (耐用)

在我們實驗室裡嚴峻的情況下, 收回. 延展   超過一萬次

Walter Goloub, Crenshaw & Bush customer service

(A) 收回在網上的負面回應
(B) 自缺陷的行李箱用己袋寄回

---

191. What does Ms. Feltham write about her luggage?

(A) She likes the color. 喜歡顏色
(B) The cases are too large. 太大
(C) She purchased the bags recently. 最近剛買
(D) The carry-on protects her samples.

登機箱保護他的樣品

192. In the review, the word "concerns" in paragraph 2, line 1, is closest in meaning to

*review n. 評論

(A) arrangements. 安排
(B) reservations. 預約, 保留意見, 異議
(C) experiences. 經驗 (反對意見)
(D) features. 特徵. 特色

193. What does Mr. Goloub offer to Ms. Feltham?

(A) A full set of Silver Ice luggage.
(B) A full set of Elegant Slate luggage.
(C) A large Silver Ice suitcase.
(D) A small Elegant Slate carry-on.

被重新設計過更好展開和 收回

194. What must Ms. Feltham do in order to receive a gift from Crenshaw & Bush?

(A) Retract negative feedback given on a website.
(B) Send a package containing a <u>defective</u> suitcase. 有缺陷的. 不完美的
(C) Prove that she is the author of a product review. 證明他是商品使用心得 的作者
(D) Complete a survey about new products.

完成新商品的調查 / 行李的把手如何?

195. What does Mr. Goloub indicate about the handles of the suitcases?

(A) They are as large as possible for the size of the suitcase.
(B) They are less reliable than those of previous models. 比之前的型號 可靠
(C) They have been thoroughly tested. 已被徹底測試過
(D) They have been redesigned to expand and retract more easily.

GO ON TO THE NEXT PAGE.

MARIE KONDO INTERIORS

7722 West Viceroy ○ St.Paul

DECEMBER 28-29
年終清倉拍賣
ANNUAL YEAR-END
CLEARANCE SALE
*clearance
/ˈklɪrəns/
n. 清除. 清倉拍賣

Phone: (502) 437-1100
Monday to Friday, 9 A.M. to 5 P.M.

① Please note that the store will close at 3:00 P.M. on Thursday, December 27 in order to prepare for the sale.

② Sales prices are available on both in-store and online purchases.

③ Sign up for Marie Kondo Interiors' VIP membership to become eligible for free delivery.

④ Our trained sales staff is available to answer any questions.

① 清注意12/27 周四. 店下午3點關門
為了準備拍賣會

② 特惠價格 店內和線上購物都通用

③ 註冊成為會員. 可符合免費送貨資格

④ 我們受過訓練的員工
能夠回答任何問題

Floor coverings
10% off
———
Window furnishings
10% off 傢具
設備
———
Bedroom & living room furniture
25% off
———
Kitchen & dining room furniture
25% off
———
Home décor items
40% off

*eligible adj. 有資格的
out legal 合格的
law
→ He is eligible for retirement.
→ Only citizens are eligible to vote.
→ to be eligible for sth.
to do sth.

To: All employees

From: Gail Gossamer

Subject: Schedule

Date: December 1

①.記錄存貨
②標價

To all employees,

12/7晚上我們要增加夜班，需要員工③搬東西和商品

We are adding an overnight shift on December 27 and
will need employees to record inventory, mark prices,
③
and move goods and merchandise. I have arranged a
或要安排一個
特別的招待   所以所有的志願者可以
special treat from Stump's so that all volunteers will
吃早餐   除了 輪班給的 津貼
have breakfast in addition to time-and-a-half pay during
the shift. Please notify me by December 7 if you are
available.

overtime premium 獎金,津貼
over time rate of pay

Sincerely,

Gail Gossamer   *商品
Store Manager   goods   article 物品
                  merchandise

ware 上市待賣的商品
freight (船,飛機)運的貨物
ie,
commodity 日用品
→ smuggled goods / articles 走私貨品
inward and outward articles
→ She had several articles of clothing
in her bag. 包內有幾件衣物

GO ON TO THE NEXT PAGE.

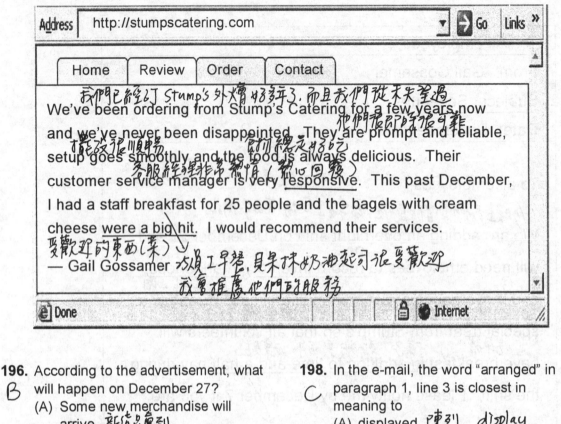

Address http://stumpscatering.com ▼ → Go Links »

Home | Review | Order | Contact

我們已經訂 Stump's 外燴好多年了，而且我們從未失望過
We've been ordering from Stump's Catering for a few years now
他們很即時很可靠
and we've never been disappointed. They are prompt and reliable,
擺設沒很順暢   食物總是好吃
setup goes smoothly and the food is always delicious. Their
客服經理非常熱情（很快回覆）
customer service manager is very responsive. This past December,
I had a staff breakfast for 25 people and the bagels with cream
受歡迎的東西（菜）
cheese were a big hit. I would recommend their services.
為員工早餐，貝果抹奶油起司很受歡迎
— Gail Gossamer
我會推薦他們的服務

Done   🔒 🌐 Internet

---

196. According to the advertisement, what
B will happen on December 27?
(A) Some new merchandise will 新貨品會到
arrive.
(B) A store will close early. 早關門
(C) A membership program will
begin. 會員活動開始
(D) A furniture sale will take place. 舉行傢具拍賣

197. What does Ms. Gossamer ask
A employees to do? 準備年度活動
(A) Prepare for an annual event.
(B) Pay attention to details. 注意細節
(C) Attend some training sessions. 參加訓練活動
(D) Demonstrate an assembly
process. 展示一個組裝過程

timeliness
n. 及時、適時
→ In journalism, timeliness and accuracy
should be equally important.

貨運準時到貨

198. In the e-mail, the word "arranged" in
C paragraph 1, line 3 is closest in
meaning to
(A) displayed. 陳列   display
(B) positioned. 定位   position
(C) planned. 計劃   plan
(D) adjusted. 調整   adjust

199. How many employees responded to
B Ms. Gossamer's request?
(A) 10.
(B) 25.
(C) 40.
(D) 100.

線上評論何者沒提及

200. What is NOT mentioned in the online
D review? 食物的品質
(A) The quality of food.
← (B) The timeliness of delivery.
(C) The level of customer service.
(D) The competitiveness of the price.
價格的競爭力

Stop! This is the end of the test. If you finish before time is called, you may go
back to Parts 5, 6, and 7 and check your work.

New TOEIC Speaking Test

Question 1: Read a Text Aloud

《 5 》 Question 1

Directions: In this part of the test, you will read aloud the text on the screen. You will have 45 seconds to prepare. Then you will have 45 seconds to read the text aloud.

比必需起床的時間還要早起,是有些掃興的。

There's something disappointing about waking up earlier

早上的時候睡睡醒醒的感覺也許不錯

than necessary. It may be nice to doze in and out of sleep in

但若你無法再次睡著會覺得超級不開心

the early morning hours, but it's especially upsetting if you

有些特定的情況會引起早上的打擾(睡不好了)

cannot fall back asleep. There are specific conditions, including

包含,睡太多和心情混亂。

a fair number of sleep and mood disorders, which might cause

early morning disturbances.

* disappointing   * doze   * upsetting   * specific
adj.令人失望的   v.打瞌睡   使心煩意亂   adj.特殊的
掃興的   特定的

* disorder   * 失眠 insomnia
n.混亂.無秩序   * a fair size
                                                   amount
* disturbance   number
n.擾亂.打擾.混亂   distance
                                                   way

PREPARATION TIME
00 : 00 : 45

RESPONSE TIME
00 : 00 : 45

GO ON TO THE NEXT PAGE.

Question 2: Read a Text Aloud

((♪ 5))) **Question 2**

Directions: In this part of the test, you will read aloud the text on the screen. You will have 45 seconds to prepare. Then you will have 45 seconds to read the text aloud.

緊接著情人節之後的時間,是結婚夫妻離婚的熱門時間。

The period immediately following Valentine's Day is a popular

有個最近的研究顯示

time for married couples to call it quits. One recent study suggested

離婚申請在這個節日之後提高 40%

divorce filings rose by as much as 40 percent right after the holiday.

過去這兩年以來我們看到平均 40% 的離婚請求律師數量

Over the past two years we've seen an average increase of 40

提升,在情人節左右

percent in the number of requests for divorce lawyers around

Valentine's Day, compared to the previous six months.

和情人節前六個月比起來。

＊ compare n. The view is beyond compare.
　　　　　　景色無與倫比

　　　　v. 比照. 比較. 比作 + with/to
　　He compared the girl to the moon in the poem.
　　　　他在詩中把女孩比作月亮

PREPARATION TIME
00 : 00 : 45

RESPONSE TIME
00 : 00 : 45

70

Question 3: Describe a Picture

 Question 3

Directions: In this part of the test, you will describe the picture on your screen in as much detail as you can. You will have 30 seconds to prepare your response. Then you will have 45 seconds to speak about the picture.

PREPARATION TIME
00 : 00 : 30

RESPONSE TIME
00 : 00 : 45

GO ON TO THE NEXT PAGE.

Question 3: Describe a Picture

*turn
→ serve one's turn
I finally had to sell the car,
but it had served it's turn.

答題範例

我最後只好把車子賣了
不過也算是物盡其用了.

《 6 》 Question 3

這個很可能是孩子的生日派對
This may be a child's birthday party.

A boy is riding a pony. 一個男孩在騎小馬

He's wearing a hat. 戴帽子

There is a woman next to him.

She appears to be leading the pony. 她好像帶領著這匹小馬

She is wearing shorts and a shirt. 穿短褲 和汗衫 shirt

I don't see any other kids around. 沒看到附近有其他
小孩

The party is probably for the kid on the pony.
→可能是為小馬上的男孩辦的

He doesn't look too enthusiastic about the situation.
對於這個情況他看起來沒什麼熱情 enthusiastic adj. 熱情的
/ɪn,θjuzɪ'æstɪk/

n. 汗衫. 襯衫
女用(份另外)襯衫

They've dressed up the pony.
打扮了小馬

It's wearing a party hat and something on its neck.
有戴派對帽·有些東西
在脖子上

I feel bad for the pony. 為小馬感到抱歉

It's probably summer. 可能是夏天

It's during the day. 在白天

It looks like a nice time for a party. 看起來是適合辦派對的時機

坦白說, 我不明白派對上有小馬的吸引人之處
To be honest, I don't understand the attraction of ponies at

birthday parties. 每個有小馬·我參加過的派對·結局都不好
Every party with a pony I've ever been to ended badly.

(21) 小孩最後都一直哭·因為某個小孩·通常生日的男孩/女孩
Kids always wind up crying because one kid, usually the birthday

boy or girl, won't get off the pony and give others a turn.
不會下馬、也不給別人機會·

72

Questions 4-6: Respond to Questions

 **Question 4**

Directions: In this part of the test, you will answer three questions. For each question, begin responding immediately after you hear a beep. No preparation time is provided. You will have 15 seconds to respond to Questions 4 and 5 and 30 seconds to respond to Question 6.

Imagine that a pollster has asked you to participate in a survey about sports. You have agreed to answer some questions in a telephone interview.

Question 4
Do you play any sports?

RESPONSE TIME
00 : 00 : 15

Question 5
How much sports do you watch on TV?

RESPONSE TIME
00 : 00 : 15

Question 6
What do you like or dislike about sports?

RESPONSE TIME
00 : 00 : 30

GO ON TO THE NEXT PAGE.

Questions 4-6: Respond to Questions

答題範例

🎧 **Question 4**

Do you play any sports? 你運動嗎？

Answer

> I play some sports. 我有時運動
>
> I enjoy baseball and basketball. 喜歡棒球和籃球
>
> I also enjoy swimming. 我也喜歡游泳

🎧 **Question 5**

How much sports do you watch on TV? 你在電視上看多少體育活動

Answer

> → We meet every so often.
>
> Not that much. 不太多　　我可能偶爾會看球賽
>
> I might watch a ball game every so often.
>
> I also watch the Olympics. 我也看
>
> 奧林匹亞運動會
>
> 偶爾
> every so often
> every now and then
> from time to time
> once in a while

Questions 4-6: Respond to Questions

＊ enjoy @ tV-ing
　　　㋡ 有權利.益. → We enjoy free medical care.
I enjoy good health. 身體健廉

（（6 ））Question 6

＊ physical /`fɪzɪk!/ adj. 身體的　③ enjoy oneself

What do you like or dislike about sports?
你喜歡或不喜歡運動的什麼？
　　　　　　　　　　　　　　→ Are you enjoying yourself?
　　　　　　　　　　　　　　你玩得高興嗎？

Answer

嗯,我想基本上是好的
Well, I think they are basically good.
　　　　　　　　　　　　　　　　　我喜歡真的運動
I like playing sports rather than watching.　而不是光看

I enjoy the exercise. 我喜歡運動

那就是運動的意義.對嗎？
That's the point of sports, isn't it?

The <u>physical</u> <u>exertion</u>. 消耗體力 （上）（下）

The competition. 有比賽

我不喜歡運動的是它現在變得很商業化
What I dislike about sports is how commercial they've

become.
　　　　運動員荒謬地的被付太多錢了
Athletes are <u>ridiculously</u> overpaid.

But (so) is everyone on TV, so that's why I never watch it.
↳錢太多　　每個在電視上的人也是這樣,
　　　　　　所以我不看。

＊ exertion
/ɪg`zɝʃən/

n. 努力·費力

He was painting the gate with exertion.

Exertion of authority over others is not always wise.
以權壓人並不總是明智的

GO ON TO THE NEXT PAGE.

Questions 7-9: Respond to Questions Using Information Provided

《 5 》 Question 7

Directions: In this part of the test, you will answer three questions based on the information provided. You will have 30 seconds to read the information before the questions begin. For each question, begin responding immediately after you hear a beep. No additional preparation time is provided. You will have 15 seconds to respond to Questions 7 and 8 and 30 seconds to respond to Question 9.

tournament
/ˈtɔːnəmənt/
錦標賽
比賽

SaltCON Board Game Convention

February 15-17

喜歡跟家人和朋友一起玩桌遊嗎？
Do you like to play board games with your family and friends? Well, if you do, then come to the SaltCON Board Game Convention February 15-17 at the Sheraton Hotel in downtown Salt Lake City. Learn new games (like Ticket to Ride, Dominion, and Word on the Street), make new friends, play in tournaments—in short, have FUN!
現在註冊可以有優惠價
Register now at www.saltcon.com for reduced rates—you can attend one, two, or all three days. Individual and group (family) rates available. Come join us at SaltCON: "Bringing the flavor back to gaming." Call the SaltCON hotline for more details (800)456-7890

把桌遊戲的味道帶回來（重新喜歡上遊戲）

Hi, I'm interested in the convention. Would you mind if I asked a few questions?

flavor
n.味道.風味   v.調味

→ She flavored the fish with sugar and vinegar.
用糖和醋給魚調味。

PREPARATION TIME
00 : 00 : 30

Question 7	Question 8	Question 9
RESPONSE TIME	RESPONSE TIME	RESPONSE TIME
00 : 00 : 15	00 : 00 : 15	00 : 00 : 30

Questions 7-9: Respond to Questions Using Information Provided

答題範例

((6)) **Question 7**

When does the event take place?

這個活動何時舉行

Answer

會議 2/15 開始

The conference begins on February 15.

It's a three-day event. 3日的活動

It ends on February 17. 2/17 结束

((6)) **Question 8**

What kind of activities will take place? 會有什麼活動？

Answer

你可以學新的遊戲

Well, you can learn new games.

You can compete in tournaments. 可以參加比賽

You can make new friends who share your interest in

board games. 可以交新朋友和你共享桌遊的興趣

GO ON TO THE NEXT PAGE.

Questions 7-9: Respond to Questions Using Information Provided

*reduce
v. ①. 減少

Question 9
② 迫使: Poverty reduced him to begging. 貧窮使他行乞
③ 把…歸納, 合併: He reduced all the questions to one.
把問題歸為一個

How can I register for the event?

我該如何申請這項活動?

④ 使降級: The officer was reduced to the ranks.
軍官被降為士兵

Answer

你可以在我們網站上申請, 得到便宜的價格
You can register for reduced rates on our website.

(U)
It's Saltcon.com.

You can attend one, two, or three days.

我們提供特別的個人, 團體價
We offer special individual group rates.

依照你的喜好   你可以網上註冊, 省下很多現金
Depending upon your preferences, you can save a lot

of cash by registering on the website.

Otherwise, you can just show up and pay at the door.
不然的話, 你可以直接在門口付錢

If you're definitely planning to attend, I'd visit the
adj. 明確地   如果你肯定有計劃要參加
肯定地
website.

You still have plenty of time to register. 你仍有許多時間申請

We hope to see you there!

count on 依賴 (偏心理意願)
→ You can't count on the train to arrive on time.

Question 10: Propose a Solution

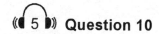 **Question 10**

Directions: In this part of the test, you will be presented with a problem and asked to propose a solution. You will have 30 seconds to prepare. Then you will have 60 seconds to speak. In your response, be sure to show that you recognize the problem, and propose a way of dealing with the problem.

In your response, be sure to
- show that you recognize the caller's problem, and
- propose a way of dealing with the problem.

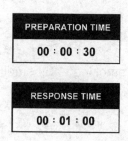

GO ON TO THE NEXT PAGE.

Question 10: Propose a Solution

答題範例

Voice Message

*tow 拖吊
*ferrace

*flame → A flame of anger lighted in his heart.
n.火焰 光亮 情緒   他怒火中燒

n.太陽台,露台

你們曾經幫助過我,反正

Hello, this call is for Phillip's Towing Service. Yes, this is

我剛發生意外.在Hauser路,接近Terrace公園的地方

Bill Greer—you guys have helped me out before—anyway, I've

我的車損壞很嚴重   我離開車道並撞上樹

been involved in an accident on Hauser Road, out near Terrace

你到了就會看到了

Park, and my car is damaged pretty bad. I ran off the road and

沒有人受傷但車子動不了

into a tree, but you'll see that when you get here. Nobody's

除了在下雨之外.車子在冒煙.我聞到汽油味

hurt but the car is not going anywhere. Aside from the fact

我在想我是否該離開車 x2/

that it's raining, the car is smoking and I smell gasoline. I'm

我沒看到任何火焰.但是煙很濃,總之,請儘快回覆我

wondering if I should get out of the car. I don't see any flames

but the smoke is pretty thick. Anyway, please get back to me

ASAP. My number is 654-1234.

Question 10: Propose a Solution

*description
n.描寫
敘述.形容

* vague
re'
adj.
不明確的.曖昧的

答題範例

*exactly
x
adv. 確切地
精確地
正確地

Hello, Mr Greer.

This is Phil from Philip's Towing. → That's exactly what I expected.

I'm sorry I missed your call. 不好意思我沒接到你的電話
正好是我所期待的

聽起來你讓自己陷入問題中
Sounds like you've got yourself a problem there.

Of course, I remember you. 當然.我記得你

You drive that green BMW, right? 你開綠色 BMW 對嗎?

Anyway, I'm calling you back. 總之.我會回電給你

Tell me <u>exactly</u> where you're at and I can send one of my boys

over right away. 告訴我你確切的位置.我馬上派小弟過去

Your <u>description</u> is a bit <u>vague</u>, but that's OK.
你的描述有些模糊.但沒關係.

Don't worry, we'll take care of the problem. 別擔心.我們會處理

Now, if you hear this message, I need you to do me a favor.

Get out of the car. 我需要你幫我個忙.離開車子

首先   我不知道損害多嚴重
First of all, I have no idea how bad the damage is.

smash 粉碎.打碎
There's hitting a tree and then there's <u>smashing</u> into a tree.

The one thing I know: smoke and gasoline are not a good match.
我知道一件事.   煙和汽油不是個好的組合

So again, get out of the car and (as) far away from it (as) possible.

Then call me back as soon as you can. 離開車子能多遠就多遠

Talk to you soon. 你有空回電給我

GO ON TO THE NEXT PAGE.

Question 11: Express an Opinion

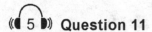

Directions: In this part of the test, you will give your opinion about a specific topic. Be sure to say as much as you can in the time allowed. You will have 15 seconds to prepare. Then you will have 60 seconds to speak.

The increasingly rapid pace of life today causes more problems than it solves. Do you agree or disagree with this statement? Give reasons and examples to support your opinion.

現今生活快速步調的增加,造成的問題比解決的更多
你對於這個陳述同意/不同意?
給出理由和例子來支持你的意見。

＊ increasingly
adv. 漸增地
　　越來越多地

＊ rapid
adj. 快的·迅速的
　　險峻的

PREPARATION TIME
00 : 00 : 15

RESPONSE TIME
00 : 01 : 00

→ The old man had difficulty climbing the rapid ascent.

82

Question 11: Express an Opinion

答題範例

Question 11

This statement is _fundamentally_ incorrect.
這個論述基本上是不正確的 → 根本地, 徹底地

There is _no doubt_ that technology has improved the quality of life.
科技有改變生活的品質這件事是毫無疑問的

Life now is easier and safer, and it's _thanks to_ technology. *thanks to*
現代生活更便利·更安全, 都是託科技之福   由於, 幸虧, 託~之福

Can you imagine our lives without electricity?
你可以想像沒有電的生活嗎?

What about the Internet and computers? Cars and planes?
還有網路, 電腦, 車子和飛機呢?

Can you imagine traveling for hundreds of kilometers on a donkey or on a camel?
你可以想像用驢子或駱駝旅行好幾百公里嗎?   / kæml /

Without technology, our lives would be harder, slower and less enjoyable.
沒有科技, 我們的生活會更艱難, 更慢比較不好玩

On the other hand, we cannot deny that technology has caused many problems.
另一方面, 我們不能否認科技引起很多問題

Pollution and health problems due to the speed of life have resulted from technology.
污染和健康問題 由於生活速度造成的 是科技造成的結果

However, these problems are correctable by more advanced technologies.
然而, 這些問題可以被先進的科技修正

For example, health problems are caused by pollution.
例如, 健康問題因為污染引起的   → v. 排除
                                                    清滅
Technology allows us to develop _treatments_ and _eliminate_ the source.   淘汰
科技讓我們發展出治療方法和消滅來源

Millions of people would die every year if not for _pesticides_. 如果沒有殺蟲劑每年會有
                                                                   幾百萬人死亡
Crops would be destroyed and diseases would spread.
作物會被破壞, 疾病會蔓延

As insects develop different defenses—technology has to constantly keep up.
如同蟲子發展出不同的防禦措施 (抗藥性), 科技必須持續地跟進

In conclusion, though technology may cause many problems, the benefits of
總而言之, 雖然科技可能造成很多問題, 科技的好處必而無疑地超過他的缺點
technology undoubtedly overcome its drawbacks.

There are real problems that can occur due to technology.   ＊ manageable
有些真正的問題會發生因為科技   adj. 可控制的
But these problems are _manageable_ by more advanced technologies. 可管理的
但這些問題可以被更先進的科技控制.

GO ON TO THE NEXT PAGE.

New TOEIC Writing Test

Questions 1-5: Write a Sentence Based on a Picture

Question 1

Directions: Write ONE sentence based on the picture using the TWO words or phrases under it. You may change the forms of the words and you may use them in any order.

＊repair
v、修理．糾正．恢復
→He tried to repair his mistake..
→It took a long time for him to repair
　　　　　　　　　　his health.

man / engine n．引擎．火車頭．工具，消防車
＋driver 火車司機
＋of warefare 武器．兵器

答題範例：The man is ⌈repairing⌉ working on the engine.
　　　　　　　　　　　　　/ ɛndʒənɪ

GO ON TO THE NEXT PAGE. →

Questions 1-5: Write a Sentence Based on a Picture

Question 2

Directions: Write ONE sentence based on the picture using the TWO words or phrases under it. You may change the forms of the words and you may use them in any order.

＊lay   **lay / brick**

ⅴ.放.擱、鋪、砌(磚)

安排. 規定：They laid down a number of rules.

賭.下注：He laid $100 on the horse.

提出：The proposal was laid before the committee.

歸(罪)於 = He laid his failure to his lack of experience.

答題範例：**The man is laying bricks.**

a brick layer.

lays bricks for a living.

86

Questions 1-5: Write a Sentence Based on a Picture

Question 3

Directions: Write ONE sentence based on the picture using the TWO words or phrases under it. You may change the forms of the words and you may use them in any order.

★tourist
n. 旅遊者." 經濟艙
adj. 旅遊的
→旅遊業 the tourist trade
industry
tourism → Tourism is growing rapidly in the area.

tourist / bus

答題範例：**Some tourists are boarding the bus.**
on the bus

GO ON TO THE NEXT PAGE.

Questions 1-5: Write a Sentence Based on a Picture

Question 4

Directions: Write ONE sentence based on the picture using the TWO words or phrases under it. You may change the forms of the words and you may use them in any order.

store / computer

*computer

+geek 電腦鬼才(不擅社交專注戀電腦的)

*store

n. 商店、倉庫 / 貯存 The grain here is for store. 此處糧食後備儲備用

豐富: He has a great store of confidence.

答題範例： **The men are in a store that sells computers.**

computer store

talking in a computer store.

v. 儲存、收存、容納

→ The cabbages were stored in the basement.

→ The barn will store five tons of grain.

Questions 1-5: Write a Sentence Based on a Picture

Question 5

Directions: Write ONE sentence based on the picture using the TWO words or phrases under it. You may change the forms of the words and you may use them in any order.

restroom / clean

✶ clean

adj. ① 乾淨的

② 未用過的: You'd better use a clean piece of paper.

③ 清白的: He was considered a candidate with a clean record.

④ 徹底的 完全的: He made a clean break with the past.

⑤ 俐落的 熟練的: The plumber did a clean job.

答題範例: **The woman is cleaning the restroom.**

       a mirror in the restroom.

    wears gloves when she cleans the restroom.

GO ON TO THE NEXT PAGE.

Questions 6-7: Respond to a written request

Question 6

Directions: Read the e-mail below.

From: Ted North <t_north@jjventures.com>
To: Andy Green <a_green@jjventures.com>
Subject: URGENT! Please Open Immediately!
Date: October 12

Andy,

如作不知道的, 我今早到達 Dallas 和客戶碰面.
As you know, I arrived in Dallas to meet the clients this morning.

然而, 航空公司弄丟我的行李. 裡面有明天會議的樣品
However, the airline lost my luggage, which contained the samples

我剛和航空公司的人掛了電話
for the meeting tomorrow. I just got off the phone with a guy from

他們找到我的行李 被送到西雅圖了
the airline; they've located my luggage—it got sent to Seattle.

不幸地是 在回到我手上之前1-3天. 行李可能在任何地方
Unfortunately, they say it could be anywhere from 1-3 days before

對我來說行不通 我需要那些
it's returned to me. That isn't going to work for us. I need those

商品樣品展示給客人看 不然的話, 我們也可能
product samples to show the client; otherwise, we might as well

取消這個會議. 你最後有可能做什麼幫忙一下嗎?
cancel the meeting. Is there anything you could do on your end to

help?

先動打謝打你囉!
Thanks in advance,

Ted North

Lead Sales Representative, Southwest Region

JJ Ventures, Inc.

Directions: Write back to Ted North as Andy Green. Acknowledge and

offer ONE solution to his problem. ①承諾~回告知收到

③欸~盡承謝忱

Questions 6-7: Respond to a written request

答題範例

Question 6

*determine
/dɪˈtɝmɪn/
v. 決定.
下決心. He was determined to win the game.

Ted,

很遺憾聽到關於你行李的事. 幸好航空公司已經找到你的行李

I'm sorry to hear about your luggage. At least the airline has located

既然無法決定你的行李何時會找到, 返回

your suitcase. Since it's not possible to determine when your luggage

我已經用隔日到貨寄樣品給你

will be found and returned, I've sent product samples by overnight

那樣一來, 你明天便不會雙手空空去見客戶了

shipping. That way, you will not have to go empty-handed to tomorrow's

每個商品有5個樣品和完整的(物品)說明書

meeting with the clients. There are five samples of each product as well

as complete descriptions. I sent the items by NSFW Overnight to your

包裹會在早上8:30到達 所以保證你在

hotel. The package will be delivered by 8:30 a.m. so that you are sure

在10:00的開會時會有樣品可以展示.

to have product samples to show when you speak at the 10:00 a.m.

meeting in Dallas.

Good luck,

Allen Green

J.J. Ventures, Inc.

* description
n. 描繪. 敘述. 形容.
→ He gave a description of what he had seen.
① 物品說明書
② 種類. 性質
→ In the zoo there are animals of every
description.
動物園裡有各種各樣的動物

GO ON TO THE NEXT PAGE.

Questions 6-7: Respond to a written request

Question 7

Directions: Read the e-mail below.

From: Moishe Fields <moishe@rippers.com>
To: Digger Fox <digger@remco.com>
Date: May 4
Subject: REMCO-18-0219 Shipment

Dear Mr. Fox,

晴有商品的箱子今天到了,而且裡頭有項我們沒有訂的商品, 馬上

The box containing shipment REMCO-18-0219 arrived today and

/ 吉他界合器 我馬上發現這項失誤

included an item we had not ordered: a guitar interface. I spotted this

並檢查收據   然而,收據顯示

error immediately and checked the invoice. However, it indicates that

我們被收取這項商品的全額   我們要求退還108元的

we have been charged the full amount of this item. We request the $108

差價   我假設你們想要這個接合器寄回

difference to be refunded. I assume that you would like the interface to

你們網站說有缺陷的商品或不正確的商品

be sent back to you. Your website indicates that defective products and

可以免費退回   但是沒有提供任何細節

incorrect items can be returned free of charge, but no details are

關於運送喜好(運送利)

provided regarding your shipping preferences. Please tell me how I

should proceed. 請告訴我我該如何進行(處理)

Regards,   *assume
            take   *defective   * indicate

                          adj. 有缺陷的   v. 指示,指出
Moishe Fields 假定
Ripper's Music 擔任   不完美的   象徵,暗示

            假裝   defect
                        n. 缺失點. 過失

以銷售經理身份回覆

Directions: Reply to Mr. Fields as Digger Fox, a sales manager from 為錯誤道歉並
REMCO Industries. Apologize for the mistake and inform Mr. 告知你會
Fields that you will refund his money, and give him TWO 退錢
shipping options to return the item.

給他2種退貨的貨運方式選擇.

Questions 6-7: Respond to a written request

答題範例

Question 7

* prompt
adj. 立即的
敏捷的

Mr. Fields,

我真誠的為我們的失誤造成您的不便道歉. 當然
I sincerely apologize for the inconvenience of our mistake. Of course,

我會立刻退還金額給您. 關於退回吉他接合器
I will refund your money promptly. As for returning the guitar interface,

我可以提供二個選項 可以郵寄寄回 免費
I can offer two options. First, you can return it by post, free of charge.

只要告訴店員寄「貨到付款」
Simply tell the clerk to send it Cash on Delivery (C.O.D.). Second, I

我可以安排我們其中一個貨運司機收取商品.
could arrange for one of our own delivery drivers to <u>retrieve</u> the item

從你店裡或任何你方便的地方 收回. 重新得到
from your store whenever it's convenient for you.

Please let me know which option is preferable to you. 價值當修飾 < adj.
                                                                         adv. ✓
更好的. 更合意的

Sincerely,

Digger Fox

REMCO Industries

* prefer
v. 寧可. 更喜歡

→ I prefer the quiet countryside to the noisy cities.

→ So you prefer living abroad?

⊖ 提出控告

→ He preferred a charge against the robber.
他控告那名盜賊

* preferable

adj. 更好的. 更合意的

→ Your idea is more preferable to mine.
你的主意比我的更好

GO ON TO THE NEXT PAGE.

Questions 8: Write an opinion essay

Question 8

Directions: Read the question below. You have 30 minutes to plan, write, and revise your essay. Typically, an effective response will contain a minimum of 300 words.

Should governments spend more money on improving roads and highways, or should governments spend more money on improving public transportation (buses, trains, subways)? Why? Use <u>specific</u> reasons and details to develop your essay.

政府該花更多錢在改善道路,高速公路上
或是政府應該花錢改善公眾交通工具 (巴士,火車,地鐵)
原因為何?
用詳細的理由和細節來發展 (完成) 你的文章。
　　　具體內

＊specific
adj·特殊的
　　具體的 The trouble with Tom was that he never had a specific aim in life.
　　明確的
　　特定的 Education should not be restricted to any one specific age group.

Questions 8: Write an opinion essay

答題範例

Question 8

就我而言，升級公眾交通系統常來更多好處
In my opinion, upgrading the public transportation system brings more advantages.

說，我們先來分析為何改善道路和高速公路不是個好選擇。如我們都知道的
First, let's analyze why improving roads and highways is not a good option. As we all

過去幾10年來，車子的數量大幅增加
know, the number of cars has risen tremendously in the last few decades. Building roads 道路

沒有解決交通壅塞的問題及而卻鼓勵了更多人開自己的車
does not solve the problem of traffic jams but encourages more and more people to use

而不是搭公車或地鐵　　　　　　　　　而且，投資道路，高速公路專案非常費
their own cars instead of buses and subways. Moreover, it is very expensive to invest in

　　　　　　　　　　　　　這些專案常引起更多的問題
roads and highways projects, and these projects often cause more problems. When roads

當在修路時，　　　　建設公司需封路，民眾要以走別條路
or highways are being repaired, construction companies have to close them and people

這會事到路上車太多　　　　　　　　　　　　　　因此
have to use other streets. This can cause a street to be overcrowded with cars; therefore,

很多人會卡在車陣中　　　　通勤者平均每年浪費一周時間在車陣中
a lot of people will be stuck in traffic jams. The average commuter wastes about one week

塞車也讓經濟每年損失很多金錢
each year in traffic jams. Traffic jams make the economy lose a lot of money each year.

車子在車陣中動彈不得　　　　但是持續排放有害氣體
Cars in traffic jams cannot move, but they continue to emit harmful smoke, which will make

the global warming issue more severe. 會讓全球暖化議題更為嚴重　　alleviate
　　　　　　　　　　　　　　　　　　　　　　　　　　　to, light v.
另一個升級公眾交通的原因是這樣可以和緩（減輕）環境問題
Another reason why upgrading public transit services is preferable is that it alleviates

如果我們有好的公眾交通工具　　　　　　δ jɪe
environmental problems. If we have good public transportation, more and more people

好多的人會使用公車或者地鐵而不是車子　交通量會減少
will use buses or subways instead of using cars. The amount of traffic will decrease;

因此　　　　　將會有比較少的有毒煙霧（氣體）太空氣污染，全球暖化的主要原因
therefore, there will be less harmful smoke, the main cause of air pollution and global

　　　　　　　　除此之外，我們需要知道政府在為人民工作
warming, in the air. Furthermore, we have to know that governments work for the people.

很多在中或低階層的民眾，大部分的人口
Many people in the middle and lower classes, who account for a large portion of the

　使用大眾交通工具因為花費少　　　　如果我們蓋更多道路
population, use public transportation because the cost is low. If we build more roads, only

只有上階層的人可以得到好處　　　　　　一個好的政府，是個會服務人民的
people in the upper class can benefit from this. A good government is a government that

政府　　　　　　不只服務一小群有錢的個體　　　　　如果人們使用巴士或者
serves all people, not only a small group of wealthy individuals. If all people use buses or

地鐵，他們會發展好的社區意識
subways, they will develop a sense of community.

這些就是為何我認為政府該專心改善公眾交通
Those are the reasons why I think governments should concentrate on improving

public transportation. I use buses as much as I can. If we all use buses or subways, this

world will be a better world. 我儘量搭公車。如果我們都搭公車或地鐵
這個世界將會是個更好的世界。

95